SUNSHINE SIMPSON

Cooks up a Storm

G.M. LINTON

Illustrated by Fuuji Takashi and Asma Enayeh

USBORNE

Auntie Sharon

Dariuszkz
(aka Daz)

Granny Cynthie &
Grampie Clive

Grandma
Pepper

Mum & Dad

Readers love Sunshine!

"A book as warm and radiant as sunshine itself!"
Lisa Thompson, author of *The Goldfish Boy*

"An utterly brilliant book that had me laughing and
crying in equal measure."
Ọlá Okogwu, author of *Onyeka and the Academy
of the Sun*

"A beautiful, heartwarming hug of a book about the
power of self-acceptance. I defy anyone not to fall in love
with Sunshine!"
Hannah Gold, author of *The Last Bear*

"A delightful story that manages to be both sincerely heartfelt and
sparklingly funny in equal measure."
L.D. Lapinski, author of *The Strangeworlds
Travel Agency*

"This uplifting and charming middle-grade is warm and funny.
It puts a spotlight on the Windrush generation and has the most
wonderful grandpa! You'll love it."
A.M. Dassu, author of *Boy Everywhere*

"A huge, uplifting hug with a message that says:
be yourself; be proud of who you are."
Jen Carney, author of *The Accidental Diary of B.U.G.*

"Sunshine lives up to her name – she's charming
and hilarious."
Aisha Bushby, author of *A Pocketful of Stars*

"This is a very special book."
Serena Patel, author of *Anisha, Accidental Detective*

"Powerfu

Ra

ACC. No: 05186288

For my godmother, Coral (Honey) Palmer,
and in loving memory of Mr and Mrs Porter and Maria Ogiste

First published in the UK in 2023 by Usborne Publishing Limited, Usborne House, 83-85 Saffron Hill, London EC1N 8RT, England, usborne.com

Usborne Verlag, Usborne Publishing Limited, Prüfeninger Str. 20, 93049 Regensburg, Deutschland VK Nr. 17560

A CIP catalogue record for this book is available from the British Library.

ISBN: 9781801313353 7604/1 JFMAMJJ SOND/23

Printed and bound using 100% renewable energy at CPI Group (UK) Ltd, Croydon, CR0 4YY.

Meet my family — and welcome to my rollercoaster life!

Me (age 6)

Grandad Bobby

The Twinzies (Lena & Peter)

ELEPHANT IN THE ROOM

Have you ever played the **A-to-Z All-Around-the-World** game?

I play it like this...

I go through countries alphabetically, from A to Z, and name their capital cities.

If I'm really testing myself, I try and name a country and capital city that begin with the same letter — like Bridgetown is the capital city of Barbados, Brussels is the capital city of Belgium, and Brasilia is the capital city of Brazil. Maybe it's something about the letter B. If I can't remember what the name of the capital city is, I make up something silly like Bear Central is the capital city of

Bulgaria, or Crocodile Rock is the capital city of Cameroon.

I love learning about new places. Geography is my most favourite subject in the whole world. One day, I'd love to go travelling. From the North Pole to the South Pole and all the way to Timbuktu — I want to go **EVERYWHERE**!

Anyway, before I wander off any further…

I tried to play the A to Z game with my friends Charley, Arun and Evie in the playground one morning, at break a couple of weeks into starting Year Six. It didn't get off to the best start, as we hit a stumbling block at the very first letter.

"Canberra is definitely the capital city of Australia," I said.

"No, it's *definitely* Sydney," Evie told me.

We went back and forth until we eventually checked it out on her phone.

"Well, it should be Sydney," said Evie, in a huff, when she realized *she* was wrong. Evie shook her phone as if willing it to change the answer. Her phone's good, but not that good!

That's the trouble with Evie Evans — she knows it all. One of the things I've grown to ~~love appreciate~~ understand about Evie is that she is bossy. A bossyboots. Bossier than a pair of wellington boots that would be too big even for the giant from Jack and the Beanstalk to wear. I'm just saying.

"I don't really like this game," said Evie. "Can we play something else?"

"At least no one's going to argue about what the capital city of England is," chirped Charley.

"Good one, Charley!" said Arun, equally chirpily. I think Arun and Charley had sensed "a situation" brewing.

Arun and Charley are my absolutely bestest friends in the whole entire world. We always look out for each other, no matter what. Meanwhile, Evie and I had been patching up our friendship ever since we had a falling-out in Year Five. But sometimes, just sometimes, the plaster falls off.

Unless someone thinks the capital of England is Scotland, I thought to myself. (I didn't say it out loud, that would not be a very patchy-up kind-of-thing to say and also a bit rude.)

"Yes, let's just play something else," I said, trying to sound as bright as possible, even though all the fun had been sucked out of my new game.

"Should we talk about 'the elephant in the room', as my mum would say?" said Charley, double shuffling her eyebrows.

I looked around. We weren't in a room, we were in the playground, and there were definitely no elephants. I'd have noticed. But really, I did know **EXACTLY** what Charley meant. In morning assembly, our head teacher, Mrs Honeyghan, had given Year Six a talk about us being the oldest in the school now, and about being responsible, as the younger kids were looking up to us. She also talked about moving on. The thought of moving on made me feel quivery inside.

"High school," whispered Charley, like they were naughty words that needed to be spoken in hushed tones.

"Charley, we only started Year Six like a minute ago. I really don't want to think about high school just now," I said, feeling even more fed up.

"Is that why you've made up this babyish game for us to play, because you're a bit scared?" asked Evie.

"There is nothing babyish about geography, Evie. Geography is literally the **WHOLE** entire world!" I drew a big circle with one of my fingers to prove the point. "And, no, I'm not scared," I snorted.

Evie made a pouty doubting face, which just made me feel even worse.

"Well, Annette and Clodagh say that Year Sevens are initiated — that's high-school speak for being properly accepted — by getting their heads flushed down the disgusting school loos by the older kids," said Charley.

Annette and Clodagh are two of Charley's big sisters. They keep telling her terrifying stories about secondary school and then laughing hysterically once they're done. Charley then shares these horror stories with Arun and me, so that we can be equally terrified. Charley says, "We share everything." Sometimes, I wish we'd share a little less.

"But my biggest sister, Shannon, says that we shouldn't worry, because although the high-school loos are disgusting, no one will flush our heads down them," said Charley.

This was only ever so slightly comforting.

Arun gulped.

"Don't worry, Arun. Shannon's just graduated from university, so she's very mature and wise. And she knows lots about everything. At least she thinks she does," added Charley.

"No, no, I'm not worried about the loos — much," said Arun. "I just hope my parents let me audition for the School of Music and Dramatic Arts next month. They kind of don't mind me singing and acting now, but they see it as more of a hobby. They want me to concentrate on my 'academics' in high school." Arun yawned as he wrapped his fingers around the word "academics". "Sorry, it just brings out the snooze in me," he said.

"Well, I think 'academics' is very important," snapped Evie. "I've been doing extra tuition since I was five! And I'm definitely sitting the test for grammar school. I'm fully trained. I'm ready."

"No one says that academics, or whatever, isn't important, Evie. But can't we just enjoy Year Six while it lasts?" I was starting to get hot and itchy, scratching at my neck. My parents had already been chatting to me about what high school I might like to go to and about "focusing" on my schoolwork in Year Six for the upcoming SATs, but I was in no mood to be talking about this right now at school. "Can we *please* talk about something else for a while?" I muttered.

"Well, yes, now that we're **TOP** of the school, I suppose we can talk about anything we want and do anything we want!" said Evie, getting slightly carried away with herself.

I guess being in the top year of primary school did mean doing things that were very top-of-the-schoolish, but like, what, exactly? We now got to sit on the benches in assembly while all the other school years had to sit on the floor. I suppose that was good. Actually, that was great. But...was that it?

My parents are always telling me, "School days are the best days of your life, Sunny." So why did I feel so strange about being in Year Six? These weren't feeling like the "best days". My heart felt like it was beating ten times faster anytime anything to do with being in Year Six or going to high school was mentioned. It was as if an actual elephant was strapped to my back, weighing me down, and I couldn't shake it off no matter how hard I tried.

2

NO WORRIES

Now I look back on it, I think Evie was right. I'd taken to playing my geography game as a distraction from all the things that were bugging me, like thinking about high school.

It felt as if there were worry worms in my tummy, tangling themselves into one giant knot. Sometimes, little butterflies excitedly fluttered and danced, too. But the worms were always trying to eat the butterflies.

As I thought it might help, I started writing a list of my worries in a new notebook. You see it on telly, don't you, when people keep a diary and tell it all their secrets? Well, I called my secret book, my **No Worries** book. It's an "ironic" title because it means the opposite of how I am really feeling. At least I think that's what ironic means. Anyway, I was very pleased with my clever title, especially as it should have put my parents off the scent if they ever found where I'd hidden it (stuffed at the bottom of my wardrobe, underneath a shoebox where I put all my old drawings that I like and want to keep). I really didn't want them to know I was worried. They worried about us all enough already, especially after my Grandad Bobby died in the summer.

I kept my **No Worries** book alongside my **Things and Places of Interest** notebook, where I write down new things and experiences, like if I meet someone from a place I've never heard of. When I first met Evie, at the beginning of Year Five, I wrote down that she'd moved to where I live in the West Midlands from an area in England called the Home Counties, which I'd never heard of before. Another place to visit when I'm older! My **Things and Places of Interest** book is full of fun notes and plans for the future. My **No Worries** book is not.

These are some of the things I jotted in my **No Worries** book (not in any particular order of worriedness):

1. I'd been at Beeches Primary School since I was five years old. Exactly half of my life. That's a long time! Apart from my family, my classmates and teachers were the people who I saw the most every day. As much as school could get on my nerves, I wasn't sure I was ready to swap it for another, especially high school — or "BIG school" as my parents like to call it. Making high school sound even bigger wasn't helping. This brings me to worry number two.

2. High school was around the corner. Not literally around the corner, I'd need to take a bus. It was just the thought that after this school year, I would be swimming (maybe drowning) in a stormy sea filled with older kids who may or may not want to flush my head down a disgusting high school loo! From **TOP** of the school to the **BOTTOM** of the sea (or toilet).

3. I was dreading having to catch a bus to school. The thought of travelling on a bus without my parents was scary. Suppose I missed my stop and didn't know my way back? The grown-ups in my family spend half of their lives complaining about public transport. How it never turns up on time, is too full, too smelly, too fast, too slow, too noisy, so I didn't want to be driving around on a bus for longer than I had to. The other half of grown-ups' lives is spent complaining about the weather. (I hope I can find something more interesting to talk about when I'm a grown-up.)

4. I desperately wanted a mobile phone, but **MY MOTHER** said I **COULDN'T** have one until **MAYBE "BIG"** school. So now I had to be in a hurry to get to Year Seven, which after suffering the trauma of Charley's flush-your-head-down-a-loo stories, I actually wasn't very much in a hurry to get to.

5. Before I could even get to secondary school, there would be tests. Tests to check how we were doing during the school year and tests for some of the schools we'd be trying to get into. Tests + tests = more

tests and **NO FUN**. I can't help but say this: these were testing times.

Don't get me wrong, I know that lots of kids look forward to starting secondary school or high school or big school or whatever you want to call it, but I was starting to realize that I wasn't one of them. Too much had changed in my world already and I just needed change to stop for a bit.

I wanted to go back to a time when my Grandad Bobby was well, when I only worried about smaller things, like what to pack in my lunch box or whether to wear tights or socks to school, instead of worrying about bigger things like what on earth we'd do without Grandad.

And, as for my mum, she'd been starting to behave a little strangely. So quiet and distant. At first, she'd just kept going as usual after we'd lost Grandad, but something about her, lately, seemed different. Mum was quickly becoming my newest worry.

"Worry is a ghost that jumps out at you, shouts 'boo', then won't stop following you. You have to turn round and face it — and shout 'boo' right back in

its face!" Grandad Bobby said that to me once. Whenever I felt scared or worried, he'd wrap me up in one of his great big hugs and say just the right thing to make me feel better. But now Grandad wasn't here to talk to about my worries, I'd have to deal with all of these changes and new things by myself. Without his words and hugs to warm me I was nervous. Actually, scared stiff.

Why did things have to change?

3

TWINKLE FLAKES

I only realized it was the start of October when the air suddenly turned colder and I let out a shiver. To be fair, this sudden drop in temperature could have been caused by two other things:

1. The dripping (I'll explain this in a bit).

2. The chilly atmosphere when I tried to sneak into the kitchen during breakfast. (The sneaking in was also related to the dripping.)

Dad was speaking in a hushed voice to Mum as she was standing at the sink. They'd both been doing this a lot recently. *Whisper, whisper, whisper.* There was something definitely going on that they didn't want to talk about in the open. Mum was looking out of the window, not at Dad. She didn't seem happily distracted by the changing colours of autumn in the garden. Her body was as rigid and as stiff as a brick.

Dad broke away from Mum, maybe because she was ignoring him. He didn't notice me but started clucking around my little brother and sister like a hen, filling their glasses with orange juice and offering them the Twinkle Flakes cereal that Mum keeps at the back of one of the top cupboards for "emergency situations". Twinkle Flakes are probably called Twinkle Flakes because each delicious crunchy bite is covered in a layer of twinkly sugar. If the Twinkle Flakes had been released from their emergency-cupboard prison, then something was definitely up.

Peter and Lena (or **The Twinzies** as I like to call them because they're twins) were not reading the room, as usual. They were giggling like they'd fallen head first into a bucket full of Twinkle Flakes – which, judging by the size of the bowls that Dad was pouring the cereal into, wasn't far wrong.

The Twinzies looked up from their sugar-coated frenzy

and stopped mid-chew when they saw me.

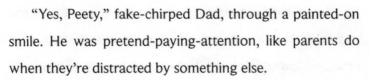

"Vy iz Sunshy soaking vet?" asked Peter through a mouthful of cereal, as I tried to sneak into the room unnoticed.

"Yes, Peety," fake-chirped Dad, through a painted-on smile. He was pretend-paying-attention, like parents do when they're distracted by something else.

Lena pointed a jabby finger in my direction. "Sunny has a rain cloud over her head. She's making a puddle on the floor."

Dad, still fake smiling, followed Lena's pointy finger — and saw me. "Sunny, you're soaking wet!"

Mum broke from her sink trance and swung herself around. "What in the world? Sunshine, what happened to you?"

"I was trying to get a stain out of my school jumper," I said, calmly.

"By throwing a bucket of water over yourself?" said Mum, in that Mum way of hers.

"No, of course not!" I made a face to indicate that Mum was sounding completely over the top. "I stood in the shower. I thought it would be quicker, but the rest of me got caught in the gush." I felt my face heating up at how dumb that sounded, and even dumber that I'd done it.

Mum and Dad's mouths fell open.

"I couldn't find a fresh jumper in my chest of drawers, and I didn't want to disturb you, so I was just on my way to grab one from the basket in the utility area," I explained.

That was true. Breakfast is usually at lightning speed in our house. A whirlwind of feeding, watering, getting dressed and then out the door so that we all get to school on time. Something was making my parents stressed, and I hadn't seen them this stressed since...since we lost Grandad, so I thought I'd help myself. And in the process of helping myself, just stress them out a bit more, it seemed.

Despite my very sensible explanation, the temperature felt like it had fallen another couple of degrees. I started to shiver a little, as if I needed two jumpers now. As it happens,

I needed a whole new change of outfit, thanks to the force of our power shower.

Mum and Dad looked at each other again and…

…burst out laughing.

Mum shook her head at me wearily. "Come on, let's get you sorted." Mum stepped over the sizeable puddle I'd made on the tiles. "And no Twinkle Flakes tomorrow, Peter and Lena. There's far too much excitement around here already."

"But they're full of so much—" Peter started.

"Sugary yumminess," Lena finished.

"Precisely," said Peter, nodding at Lena in a very satisfied way as they clinked their spoons together in celebration.

Mum looked at Dad and raised an eyebrow. Dad shrugged and smiled a goofy smile at her as he grabbed the bucket and mop. That smile of Dad's always works a treat on Mum.

At least the temperature had warmed up a bit.

"Good as new," said Mum as she patted down my clean — and dry — uniform ten minutes later.

"Mum, is everything okay?" I asked.

Mum raised her eyebrows. If eyebrow-raising was a championship sport, Mum would be a gold medallist. "Of course everything's okay. Everything's just fine."

But her answer didn't make me feel like everything was okay.

Because if that were true, then why were she and Dad constantly whispering to each other? The last time they whispered like this, it was because they didn't want to tell me that my Grandad Bobby was unwell. Whispering makes me feel very worried.

Mum put a hand on her hip. As it happens, Mum could also win any "I'm a little teapot" posing competitions. "Is everything okay with *you*?" she asked. "I know this is a big year and there are lots of changes coming up, but everything will be fine, you'll see."

"Will it, Mum?" I asked, helplessly. "What about all the tests in Year Six? What about choosing the right school? And what if I don't like high school when I get there?"

"Aw, it's natural to feel nervous, sweetie. Once we get to have a proper walk around all the schools at the open evenings in a couple of weeks' time, you'll see that big school isn't as big and scary as you're probably imagining. And Dad and I can help you with your school workbooks." Mum smiled. "Now, off you go. Dad will be waiting."

Mum had performed the oldest trick in the book. She'd turned the tables and made the conversation all about me — like adults annoyingly do when they're trying to change the subject from something *they* don't want to talk about.

4
INDEPENDENCE

Dad and **the Twinzies** were waiting for me at the front door. For the first month of Year Six I'd walked to school by myself, but ahead of Mum or Dad and **the Twinzies** so that I was in sight of them. But now we were changing the pattern around. Mum or Dad would walk **the Twinzies** to school in front of me — and I'd follow behind. This was all part of a grand dress-rehearsal for high school, and "finding my independence". Year Six were now allowed to walk to and from school on our own — as long as our parents gave their permission. Some kids did walk alone, but some parents, like mine, still wanted to keep ~~babying us~~ an eye out.

As I left the house, our neighbour, Mrs Turner, was on patrol at her front gate, "pruning her hedges". Mrs Turner's hedges are almost completely bald, so these days she just fakes the cutting action. To be fair, since we lost Grandad, Mrs Turner doesn't turn out faithfully on her doorstep every morning like she used to. I guess no one has the time to spare her more than a couple of minutes for conversation — but Grandad always did.

"Morning, Mrs Turner!" I waved, but kept moving, just in case she wanted to chat. With the bathing-in-clothing-that-isn't-swimwear incident, we were a little behind schedule. And Dad's long legs were stretching away from me.

"Glad to see you're learning a bit of independence by walking to school on your own," shouted Mrs Turner, pausing for a moment. "Children are too mollycoddled these days. I left school at fifteen, you know. And there was no idling or messing about for me. I had to go out and work for my supper."

I didn't really have time for one of Mrs Turner's "I left school at fifteen" chats. My Auntie Sharon reckons that the only jobs Mrs Turner hasn't done in her lifetime are working as a chimney sweep or with a canary down a coal mine. I had to hope that Mrs Turner's snooping abilities didn't include mind-reading powers, because all that popped into my head right then was that the canary had a lucky escape.

Risking a never-ending telling-off, I interrupted her. "Mrs Turner, I had to change my jumper this morning because I had a little mark on it and now I'm running late." Mrs Turner was delighted with this bit of information, which was a deliberate part of my getaway plan.

"Tut, tut, tut. When I was at school, I was never late. Tardiness is a stain on human character," she remarked — which made me wonder whether nosiness was a stain on human character too.

"Run along then, dear," she continued. "And tell your mother she's probably using the wrong soap powder. I'll show her the one I use later."

Mrs Turner didn't have to tell me twice, I was gone. Picking up my pace, I did a walkie-hop-jog thing and then broke into an all-out run. My parents are usually my timekeepers — "stop dawdling, Sunny", "get a move on, Sunny", "time waits for no man, Sunny" — blah, blah, blah. To my horror, I realized I had no idea what time it actually was. Why couldn't my parents see how useful and very, *very* necessary it was for me to have my own phone, so that at least I could tell the time — and make phone calls and send text messages while I was at it. I couldn't be late for school, not with Miss Fairweather, our new class teacher, waiting at the other end. She thought lateness was a stain on human character too.

On my way to school, passing the shops that lie halfway between school and home, I could see Jakub at the Polski Sklep through his shop window waving at me from his counter. I waved back at him, and then waved to Mrs Flowers, who was fixing her bouquets in their buckets outside her florist's. Next to the Polski Sklep and the florist's is Chanda's Grocery Store, which had just become our neighbourhood's post office. Mr Chanda was proudly polishing the red and white Post Office sign outside the shop. He waved a polka-dotted cloth at me.

"Any letters to post today, Sunshine?" he called.

"No thanks, Mr Chanda, I prefer email!" I joked, waving at him.

"Modern-living, eh? But you can't beat a good letter," he chortled.

Mr Chanda sounded like Miss Peach, my teacher in Year Five. I don't really like to think about the first-ever letter I sent by post. It was to my French pen pal, Elise Baptiste. I wrote it as part of Miss Peach's special letter writing project. The amount of trouble I got myself into with that letter, after writing mean things about Evie Evans in it. I know it was wrong, but I'd written them just to Elise. I didn't realize Miss Peach was going to get me to read out Elise's reply in front of the whole class!

Which reminded me, I did owe Elise a letter. I wanted to find out the latest instalment of how she and her arch-enemy Olivier Leclerc were getting on. The last time I'd heard from her, he'd accidentally fallen head first into a pigsty during a school trip to a farm. Did he jump or was he pushed? Elise didn't say in her letter.

Being out in the fresh air must have been doing me some good, because I was actually starting to cheer up a little. I love where I live. Our house, and the streets and people that surround it, even Mrs Turner. They all reminded me of Grandad Bobby — and that made me happy.

Dad was keeping a pace but gently looking back, while trying to rein in **the Twinzies**, who were tearing ahead of him.

Rounding another corner, just before the turn into school, I spotted Arun and Charley. They live in a different direction, so we now met at the old willow tree near to school and walked the last bit together. From this point, my parents were happy to carry on without keeping their eyes on me — especially because Charley had a phone to use in case of emergencies. It was just Arun and me who were phoney-no-mates.

Arun and Charley were waiting for me underneath the tree. The branches were swaying in the autumn breeze, leaves rustling, as if they were listening in on my friends' secrets, whispering them to each other. I didn't know if it was because of the noise the tree was making, but Charley and Arun didn't see me coming.

"Ahem!" I announced.

"Oh, hey, Sunny," said Charley. "We've just seen your dad go past."

"To be precise, he went past thirty-three seconds ago," declared Arun. "I set a timer to see how far you were behind him on MY NEW PHONE!" Arun waved the phone around proudly, like it was made out of gold dust.

The phone flashed at me with bright lights and screamed:

ALERT! ALERT! SUNSHINE SIMPSON IS THE LAST PERSON WITHOUT A PHONE!

Well, that's what was playing out in my head.

Arun had a phone? We had been practically the last kids in our class without one. Now, I was virtually on my own — literally! Charley got her phone in the summer holidays for her tenth birthday. That hadn't bothered me too much at the time, because everything was still so freshly impossible without Grandad. But this latest news was too much for me. It rocked me down to my school shoes.

"Are you okay, Sunshine? You're face looks all squished up, like you're in pain," said Charley.

I was in pain, but not physical pain. I said nothing in reply, too mesmerized by the beauty of Arun's phone to speak.

Charley was still looking at me in a very concerned way. "Do you feel sick?"

I nodded my head but remained silent.

"Do you have a headache?" Charley continued.

I nodded again.

"Hmm...I wish I had one of my mum's books with me just in case it's something really dangerous!" she said cheerily.

Charley's mum is a nurse, so in Charley's mind this makes her a nurse too.

Sadly, for Charley — and luckily for me — there was nothing dangerously wrong with me apart from my bad mood. Arun was **NOT** supposed to get a phone until his eleventh birthday in January, and I would hopefully follow on my eleventh birthday in March. That was the plan. He was **WAY** too early.

"I know I'm not supposed to get a phone until my birthday," he said, as if reading my mind. "Mum and Dad have treated me early because they say they're 'proud of me and trust me'. They also think the phone will come in useful if we ever need to contact each other urgently while I'm at Star Makers."

Following his brilliant performance in the Year Five school showcase in the summer, Arun's parents had let him join performance arts classes at STAR MAKERS THEATRE CLUB.

What Arun had said about his parents suddenly made me wonder whether my parents were proud of – or trusted – me. But Arun's smile was so broad and so genuine, I felt my outrage seep out of me and trickle into the nearby drain.

"Ah, that's better," smiled Charley. "Your face has gone back to normal. I was starting to think we'd have to call a doctor."

"Well, it's a good job you both have phones, if you'd needed to make the call," I said. I could feel my whole body wilting like an un-watered sunflower, all droopy with disappointment. If only my parents were with us at that very moment to witness that I also needed a phone in case of emergency.

"Your phone looks great, Arun," I said, finally remembering my manners. It wasn't actually Arun or Charley's fault that I was a sad loser who was now the new Mayor of Loserville.

"What looks great?" I heard a voice trill from behind me. This was all I needed. Now Evie would see I was a loser too!

"Hi, Evie," I said. There was no point in pretending, so I just spat it out. "Arun has a new phone."

"Let's see!" Evie's trill hit new levels of sound-defying gravity. She whipped her own phone out of her bag to compare the two. Then Charley added her phone into the mix. It was like the technology had taken over their brains; they all huddled around cooing in delight over their treasures.

The rest of the way to school, Arun, Charley and Evie excitedly compared their blah-blah-blahs to their do-dah-dahs. It's not that I wasn't listening, it's just that I didn't understand all the things they were saying because **I DIDN'T HAVE A PHONE OF MY OWN!** I felt like I was blazing red from the insides out. To anyone passing by, it probably looked like my friends were walking to school alongside a giant, angry tomato.

"Don't worry, Sunny. You'll get a phone soon," said Evie, brightly. "Of course, I've had a phone since the end of Year Four, probably because I've always been the oldest and most mature person in my year group. And I suppose I'm the oldest kid in the whole school now, aren't I, as we're in Year Six and my birthday's on the first of September? I'm top of the top of the entire school! Can you believe that?"

I gritted my teeth so tightly that I'm sure not even water could have passed through them.

As we walked through the school gates, Dad was hurrying out, as **the Twinzies'** class starts five minutes earlier than mine. "Oh, there you are, slowcoach," he said.

"I almost got worried for a minute, but then I remembered, Charley has a phone to use if there's an emergency." Dad patted me on the head. "Have a good day!" Then he got his own phone out of his pocket and walked off.

Oof! Why is life so unfair?

5

RIGHT ON TRACK

Person of the Day: The British historian David Olusoga OBE knows a lot of things about the past. He's a really clever professor of Public History who talks and writes about how we used to live.

As we went into class, I tried to ignore the sound of everyone plopping their phones into the basket kept by Miss Fairweather's desk. At least that was something. No one was allowed to keep their phone during the school day — so at least I wouldn't feel like a complete alien.

I kept my focus on what Grandad Bobby might have said to shake me out of my pit of despair. "Keep your chin up and your temper down." So that's exactly what I did.

I must have looked very strange walking to my desk with my chin jutted upwards and outwards, especially when I tripped over Marcus Cruickshank's chair and travelled faster than lightning to my seat. That's the problem when you have feet the size of mine, they get in the way **A LOT**, especially when you're not looking where you're going.

"Ah, just what I like to see! Walking through any obstacle to get on with your learning! I approve. Well done, Sunshine Simpson!" said Miss Fairweather, taking in a deep sniff of air with satisfaction. Her nostrils quivered like there was an ill wind blowing. "I've never had any class get less than top marks in their end of year exams — and I'm not about to start now. If we all follow Sunshine's example, we'll be right on track by the time you get to the SATs in May."

I felt myself burning up, not only with embarrassment, but also from the hot glares of some of my classmates, searing right through the back — and front — of my head. What could be worse than being a teacher's pet? Well, apart from not having a phone.

Miss Fairweather joined the school at the start of term. She is completely different to Miss Peach, who was my teacher in Year Five. Let's put it this way:

Miss Peach = sweet, miaowing kitten.

Miss Fairweather = fierce, ROARING lion.

Nothing gets in Miss Fairweather's way. She walks with her back straight and her head held high. She'd probably walk through a field of booby traps without looking down. This woman has no fear. Miss Fairweather used to be a physical training instructor in the army, and then a PE teacher in secondary school before she set herself "a new challenge" of "helping" primary-school children. That's probably why she mostly wears sports gear. Tracksuits and trainers and a whistle around her neck are her uniform — and boy does she put them to good use. Every morning we'd stand by the side of our desks, doing stretches and star jumps, because she believed "the rigours of exercise do wonders for the mind".

That day, Miss Fairweather stood at the front of the classroom and clapped her hands together to get our attention.

"Right, everybody," she said, pacing back and forth across the floor, like she was still in exercise mode. I wondered whether Miss Fairweather was about to ask us to drop to the floor and give her fifty push-ups, but she didn't.

"Can anyone tell me what month this is?"

Marcus Cruickshank's hand shot up. "It's October, Miss!" Marcus pushed his glasses back up his nose in satisfaction.

I could swear I detected the faintest eye roll by Miss Fairweather. "Technically, yes, it is, Marcus. Let me expand my question: what other significance does the month of October have?"

I felt myself burning up again, probably because I thought I knew the answer. But I didn't want to risk any more hot stares from my classmates, so I kept my hand down.

"Sunshine Simpson, you look like a girl with an answer up her sleeve. Tell me, what month do you think it is?" asked Miss Fairweather.

I shuffled nervously in my seat. "Um, Black History Month, Miss?"

"Precisely. The month of October in the United Kingdom is indeed Black History Month. This month, as part of our lessons, we'll be focusing on inspirational Black Britons, and each day we'll feature an inspiring example on the smart board. You can also help to choose someone by doing your own research at home."

"That's not fair, Miss!" Riley Edmunds shouted. "Sunshine has one up on us!"

Miss Fairweather raised an eyebrow. "And why would that be, Riley?"

"Sunshine did that speech on being from the Windy Run generation at the summer show, so she already knows loads of stuff."

It's true that my parents and grandparents have always

told me a lot of stuff about Black history, but I don't always take it in, so I'm no expert. There would always be lots to learn, but, clearly, Riley had even more to learn than me.

"If you mean the Windrush generation, Riley, then, yes, this is a very important part of Black British history, but there's also—"

"Slavery, Miss!" said Riley, interrupting Miss Fairweather again.

I felt myself blazing with fire then, but not from embarrassment. Before I could stop myself, I put my hand up. Miss Fairweather nodded for me to speak.

"Slavery is an important part of Black history, and there are stories about people like Ignatius Sancho and Olaudah Equiano who spoke out to abolish it, but there's also *a lot* more to our history."

"Well said, Sunshine Simpson!" said Miss Fairweather. She put her hands up to her temples and then expanded her arms as far as they would go, as if she was about to teach us a new exercise. "Open minds, open lives!"

I nodded my head vigorously, but then noticed Riley giving me evil stares. I really didn't want to make an enemy of him. We'd managed to get to Year Six without any problems, and I didn't want us to get into any beef now we'd nearly made it to the end of primary school.

Miss Fairweather rolled her head around as if it needed extra exercise (it didn't). "Right, class, let's get down to business. Textbooks out for maths, and then to relieve the pressure, we'll go for a brisk walk around the playing field at break. Nothing like a burst of air to the lungs to boost team spirits and your brain cells."

Relieve the pressure? Did Miss Fairweather actually know the meaning of the words playing and break?

Marcus Cruickshank raised his hand. "Isn't breaktime for taking a break, Miss?" Marcus wasn't trying to be cheeky — he was just being Marcus.

Miss Fairweather didn't look impressed. "A bit of structured play will help focus your minds. Year Six is a serious business, people. And I'm here to help this business succeed!"

You see, she's **FIERCE**.

The class gulped. Hard.

6
STRAINED SMILE

I was eager to get home from school to tell Dad — and Mum when she got home from work later — about what the class would be doing for Black History Month. That should loosen them up a bit, I thought. Mum and Dad love to talk about Black history and always tell us about how they were never taught it when they were at school "back in the day".

But when I walked into the kitchen, there was a strange atmosphere clinging to everything — and I don't mean the leftover smell from one of Peter Twinzie's bottom bombs, either.

Mum was home from work early sitting at the kitchen

table with Dad's mum, my Granny Cynthie. Granny had one hand on top of Mum's.

Mum pulled her hand away and smiled a strained smile at me, as if she'd swallowed a broom handle.

"Is that you home, already?" said Mum. "Had a good day?"

I could have asked Mum the same question. I was home the same time I always was — what was her excuse? I said nothing.

"Sunshine, are you okay? You seem drained," said Mum, sounding like Charley trying to diagnose me.

"You're right, she doesn't look herself," agreed Granny Cynthie.

"Are you okay, Sunshine?" repeated Mum, but louder this time.

I wasn't okay. My mouth was dry and I couldn't speak. Something felt wrong. Both Mum and Granny Cynthie waited for an explanation.

I couldn't think of one.

"Where are **the Twinzies** and Dad?" I asked instead.

"They're outside with Grampie Clive doing the

garden chores," said Mum.

Before he died, Grandad Bobby had left a list of jobs, month by month, for us to do in the garden.

FOR THE ATTENTION OF: Sunshine, Peter and Lena
IMPORTANT MISSION: Garden jobs (should you choose to accept it)

The thought of Grandad's words lit up my insides and I smiled.

"That's better." Mum smiled back at me, sympathetically. "I know there's a lot going on, but I don't want you to worry."

"All this pressure on kids these days," tutted Granny Cynthie. "Things were so different in my day. Yes, we valued education, but I don't remember all this fuss over which school we'd end up in. All these tests and choices. We went to our local parish school when we were seven and stayed there until we left school as teenagers. And we were happy with it."

I had a sudden wish to be transported back in time to Granny Cynthie's school. I'd love to stay in the same class all the way through to my GCSEs, especially if I had Arun and Charley with me. And I bet Granny Cynthie never had to worry about not being cool because she didn't have her own phone.

"Why don't you go and join the others in the garden for a little while? Get some fresh air, before starting your homework," said Mum.

All the reminders about tests and homework were starting to do my head in.

Before I went out, I remembered about the Black History Month class assignment. I swung round to tell Mum — if anything would cheer her up that would — but she was back in her huddle with Granny Cynthie at the kitchen table.

Mum had managed to distract me, yet again, by switching the attention from herself onto me. But it didn't feel like it was me that needed worrying about. I needed to find a way to work out what was going on.

7

BEN EVER-LANCE

People of the Day: Yvonne Conolly CBE came to Britain from Jamaica as part of the Windrush generation. She was only twenty-nine when she became a head teacher – and Britain's first female Black head teacher. Wales's first Black head teacher was Betty Campbell, and there's a statue of her in the centre of Cardiff to honour all her achievements.

The next day, Miss Fairweather had something to tell us. I wondered whether she'd signed us all up to run a marathon; fortunately it wasn't that. "Listen up, people! We have a guest who has something special to tell you."

The classroom door opened and, like a wonderful mirage, in came Miss Peach. She'd been promoted to assistant head teacher and she literally **suited** the part. Today, she was dressed in a smart blue **suit** and her brown hair flowed behind her, like she was walking with her own breeze.

"Being in Year Six is such an exciting time, children," she began. "You are standing just before dawn, at the break of day, with new adventures to have and new friends to meet. However, there is no doubt that this time can be very overwhelming. I've been thinking about you a lot since the start of term and I want you all to know you are not alone."

At this point I thought Miss Peach was going to tell us that she was going to do a tag team with Miss Fairweather and they'd be jointly teaching us. My biggest hope was that Miss Peach would teach us in the mornings so that we could cut out the morning star jumps and stretches.

No such luck.

"Today, I want to talk about benevolence," continued Miss Peach. "To be benevolent is to be kind and well meaning, charitable and giving — and that's the example we want to encourage you to follow as you leave Beeches Primary — benevolence."

Marcus Cruickshank raised his hand. "Is Ben Ever-Lance the patron saint of the school?"

Miss Peach looked at him softly, as if wondering what would become of him when he entered into the big, wild world of high school. Right there and then, I knew I'd miss Marcus if we ended up going to different schools.

"You're thinking along the right lines, Marcus," said Miss Peach warmly, covering up the hint of daftness in the air.

"In December, Year Six will hold a charity day, where you will host your own stalls, deciding within teams what you will sell, and raising money for a charity of your choice. This will help you with your teamwork and management skills. Reports will be sent to your secondary schools, so that your new teachers will get a well-rounded impression of you. But what's most important is, this will be FUN, FUN, FUN! And you can invite your families to join in too." Miss Peach laughed, happily.

None of the class, including Miss Fairweather, joined in with the happy laughter. Did we really need this hassle in Year Six?

Miss Peach cleared her throat and carried on. "My desire is for you to create even more wonderful memories of this school and nurture everlasting bonds. I will now leave Miss Fairweather to talk you through everything. Goodbye, children — or as our French friends across the channel would say, 'au revoir'." And with that, Miss Peach swept out of the room as gracefully as a Disney princess.

The whole class switched their attention to Miss Fairweather.

"No battle was won without teamwork, so we will rise to the challenge. Miss Fairweather NEVER FAILS!" She thumped her fist down defiantly on her desk, which made us all jump a couple of centimetres out of our seats. "Now, as there are thirty of you in the class, I'm going to split you up into six groups of five."

A wave of nervous excitement rippled through the class as we all wondered which groups we'd end up in. Of course, I was hoping to be with Arun and Charley, but not with Riley Edmunds — especially after our run-in over Black History Month the previous day. And if I ended up with Evie, would she be as bossy as ever or take a chill pill? My bet was on the first option.

Miss Fairweather pulled out a piece of paper from her desk drawer. She rolled her shoulders and did a few arm rotations before reading out the names. She explained that her and Miss Peach had set the groups in advance, as they didn't want any arguments about who was working with whom. She also said we were grouped with people who we would work well with, or who would bring out a different quality in each of us. We all held our breath. Our fate had been decided.

I dared to steal looks over at Arun and Charley. Arun was blowing furiously out of his top lip at his fringe and Charley's sky-blue eyes pretty much popped out of her head. The butterflies flittered and danced in my tummy and then got attacked by the worms. Evie didn't look worried at all.

Our names hadn't been called out by

the time Miss Fairweather got to the last two groups. But neither had Riley's or Carey Crick's (Riley's best friend).

GROUP FIVE
Seraphina Adebayo
Sheena Sandhu
Maya James
Marcus Cruickshank
Carey Crick

GROUP SIX
Evie Evans
Charley McCarthy
Arun Lal
Sunshine Simpson
Riley Edmunds

The whole class erupted into excited chatter. Well, most of the class. Riley and Carey were folding their arms and scowling. Those two were practically twins — but with different parents! Part of me felt a bit sorry for them. I was lucky to have been grouped with my friends — though I did wonder whether I'd been grouped with Evie as some kind of test after our falling-out in Year Five. Evie wore a huge grin on her face. Arun gave his fringe a break from blowing at it, and Charley's eyes went back into her head.

"Hey, miss, why don't I get to work with Carey?" questioned Riley, without putting his hand up.

Miss Fairweather gave him a look that would match one of my mother's special glares. "As I said, Riley, there will be no arguments about the groups. When you go to secondary school, you'll be meeting new people. Working with others is an opportunity to see things a bit differently."

"Well, Sunshine gets to work with her friends," grumbled Riley.

Miss Fairweather chose to ignore the comment. Instead, she had a tale of warning for the whole class. "There are ups and downs in every team," she began. "In 1997, if it wasn't for my teammate Paula Clark-Lyons being distracted at the last moment by the roars of the crowd, we would have sailed to victory in the Scottish inter-schools' championship one hundred metres relay final. Instead, the win slipped through our fingers as quickly as the baton, due to her shoddy handover to me on the last leg... Teamwork WILL make your dreams work, people! FOCUS and UNITE."

I thought about Miss Fairweather's warning about the ups and down of working in a team. Sure, Evie is bossy, but we were getting on a lot better these days. The real worry now was Riley. He was **NOT** in a good mood after being separated from Carey, and I don't think he was my biggest fan after my comments about Black history.

But Charley and Arun — well, they are pure perfection. We're the Three Musketeers. One for all and all for one. Always and for ever. With me and my buddies working in a team, what could possibly go wrong?

8

KNEES UP!

Bonus Person of the Day: Despite being set back by lots of injuries, Dame Kelly Holmes didn't give up and, in 2004, became double Olympic champion in the 800 metres and 1500 metre races – the first Briton in more than 80 years to do so.

After lunch, we had our PE lesson. Miss Fairweather decided that we should do a couple of laps of the playing field in our charity teams.

"Nothing like a jog to inspire genius," she said, as we all lined up in our groups in the playground.

"Do you think she's secretly training us for the army?" whispered Charley.

"Probably, but I don't think it's such a secret," I whispered back.

"RIGHT! Roll out, people!" Miss Fairweather blew her whistle. It pierced the air like a scream. After every ten seconds she released another group. My group was the last to set off.

"If you think I'm running with you lot, you've got another think coming," said Riley, turning to me with a scowl plastered across his face. "I'm especially not running with the teacher's pet. EAT MY DUST!" And, with that insult, he took off like a greyhound after Carey's group.

"Hmph! Your loss," muttered Charley.

"You can run, but you can't hide!" shouted Evie.

"What's his problem?" wondered Arun.

I shrugged. "Let's just think of some ideas for our stall and maybe we can win him over. If he already thinks I'm a teacher's pet, then at least I can try and live up to the name."

"Hey, that's an idea! What about a **bring your pet**

to school stall?" said Arun. "We can charge for photos to be taken with each one."

Evie shook her head vigorously. "No, no, no, no, no! That would be far too noisy and stinky."

"Okay — a **dance until you drop** stall then. Arun and I can teach everyone some Irish dancing or bhangra moves," said Charley.

"Well," said Evie, huffily, "the whole point of the charity day event is that it's about ALL of us and ALL of our talents. Even though, it's also true, that I can dance, too."

"Well, I'm sure we could all teach some moves **AND** you and Arun could also teach people to sing as a special bonus," I said.

"Hmm…I suppose it's not too much of a bad idea." Evie had suddenly changed her mind!

At that moment, Miss Fairweather dashed past. She'd lapped us. "KNEES UP! KNEES UP! KNEES UP!" she shouted. "Slackers are amateurs!"

With all that thinking about our ideas, we'd forgotten to run.

Charley, Arun, Evie and me all looked at each other and burst out laughing.

"Look, whatever we do, we've got to make it fantastic," said Charley.

Evie's mouth broke into a delicious grin. "We'll come up with a charity stall that's so good, not even someone called Charity McCharity could come up with it!"

When she wasn't being bossy, Evie could actually be quite funny. I had a new burst of enthusiasm.

"ALWAYS AND FOR EVER!" I shouted. Arun, Charley and I put our hands one on top of another.

I glanced over at Evie. She looked a bit lost, as if she didn't know what to do with herself, so I reached over and took one of her hands and put it on top of mine.

"Always and for ever?" I asked her.

"Always and for ever," she grinned.

That sealed it. Evie was officially part of our gang.

Now we'd just have to work on Riley.

9

GOING AWAY

Since Grandad passed away, Mum, Dad, **the Twinzies** and me all made an effort to eat a family meal together every evening around the dining-room table, instead of on trays, sitting on the sofa in front of the telly. Dinner time was our family talking time. Our "healing hour" as Dad liked to call it.

But that night, only part of the family was talking and that was **the Twinzies** and me. Mum and Dad had clammed up; they were being very cagey.

And then Dad said something that caught me off guard. "Listen, kids, I have to go away for a few days."

The Twinzies and I looked up from our plates.

"Just on some business," he continued. "I'm leaving in the morning, but I'll be back by Friday."

Oh, so that's why Mum and Dad had been so quiet. I couldn't remember a time when Dad wasn't at home with us. I looked across at Mum. I could tell she wasn't happy about it. If she'd been pleased, she'd have been quick to say something. But she said nothing. She just carried on picking at the food on her plate.

"Cheer up, everyone! I thought you'd celebrate getting your old dad out of the way for a few days." Dad laughed nervously, like he was being caught out telling fibs. "So how have your days been?" Dad was using the classic grown-ups' distraction technique of changing the subject. And he knew that once **the Twinzies** start talking, they couldn't stop.

"Johnny Larkin got a bit of rubber stuck up his nose during maths—" began Peter.

"And Mrs King was going to get his mum to come and fetch him to take him to A&E, but then he sneezed and it flew out of his nose and onto Davina Connelly's maths book. Then Mrs King had to pull out the page and throw it away, because it had a trail of rubber and snot all over it," interrupted Lena.

"But Davina didn't mind, because she doesn't like coded addition, and she probably would've got all the answers wrong anyway," added Peter.

"Column addition," corrected Lena. "Column addition...with an extra column made out of gooey snot."

Both Peter and Lena started laughing hysterically.

Mum didn't say anything. Usually, she'd shut down that kind of conversation faster than you can say "pass me the sick bowl". But that night she seemed distracted: in the room, but not in the room, if you see what I mean.

I put down my knife and fork. It was unfortunate that we were having green peas with our fish and new potatoes — all I could see now were pellets of green bogies on my plate.

"How about you, Sunny?" asked Dad, glossing over the snotty story. I didn't want to talk about me, I wanted to talk about Dad's disappearing act.

"Well, Sunny?" repeated Dad.

I started to tell him about the charity day, but my heart

wasn't in it. All I could think about was how sad Mum looked. I looked across the table to see her eyes had clouded over. Then she smiled at me again and excused herself, getting up from the table and leaving the room.

After the rest of us had finished our dinner, I went upstairs. Passing by Grandad's old bedroom, I noticed that the door was slightly open. Mum always kept the door firmly shut now. Grandad's room basically remained untouched since the day he left to go into hospital, like Mum was trying to trap all the memories of him inside. Maybe she thought if we left the door or window open for too long that, somehow, all our memories of Grandad would fly away.

A random, terrible thought filled my mind. Grandad wouldn't come back and haunt us and play tricks on us by leaving his door open, would he? He was always a joker… Nah, he'd know he'd frighten us out of our skins! Still, I peeked through the crack in the door, just in case.

Mum was sitting at the end of Grandad's bed. I couldn't see her face, as her body was half-turned towards the window. One of Grandad's shirts was resting across her lap. She'd been saying she was going to pack up some of his clothes for the charity shop for ages, but she hadn't done it yet. Maybe Mum had been reminded by me talking about the charity day at school?

But she didn't look like she was about to do any clothes packing; she just sat there, stiller than silence, holding onto the shirt.

I didn't know what to do. Should I go into the room or not? Should I fetch Dad? I wasn't brave enough to go in and intrude, and I didn't really want to tell Dad. Somehow that felt like I'd be telling tales on her. So, I just went to my room and shut the door quietly behind me. Leaving Mum to her faraway thoughts.

10

CODED ADDITION

Person of the Day: Formula One (F1) racing driver Sir Lewis Hamilton has worked really hard to be at the TOP of his sport. He's been world champion seven times and has also won more races than anyone else in the sport. He started driving karts when he was eight years old – and won LOADS of stuff. He's always tried to give something back, so he does a lot of charitable work to support young people from underrepresented groups in the UK.

I was still thinking about Mum when I came down to breakfast the next morning. She was just getting quieter and quieter. Usually, I'd think this was a good thing, as she can nag quite a lot, my mum. But she was making me feel uneasy, like I needed to do something to help her get back to her old nagtastic self.

Mum was sat at the kitchen table nibbling at a slice of toast and **the Twinzies** were chomping on their cereal. Dad had already left for his work trip. He'd come into our bedrooms the night before and kissed us all on the head, reassuring us that "everything's okay and I'll be back within the blink of an eye". I hoped so. Without Dad around, I felt responsible for looking after Mum.

I immediately went over to the table and cleared **the Twinzies'** cereal bowls and Mum's plate, plopping them into the sink and rolling up my sleeves. I then squeezed too much washing-up liquid onto the dishes and pushed the hot-water tap to full throttle, making the sink fill up like a bubble bath.

Three sets of eyes followed me across the room. **The Twinzies'** spoons were still held in mid-air from when I whisked their bowls away. Mum was still chewing the last bit of her toast. Well, I think it was the last bit, I didn't really check what I was scraping into the bin on my way to the sink.

"What are you doing, Sunny?" asked Mum.

Trying to stop you from being so far away, I thought.

"I'm washing up the breakfast things," I said.

"Are you feeling okay?" asked Mum.

What was with all the questions? My family really had no trust in my goodness or kindness, did they?

"I'm fine," I said. "Just giving a little back."

"A new phone won't jump out from the washing-up suds," said Peter.

Lena snickered.

"How about I dip *you* in the suds and see who jumps out then!" I shot back, between gritted teeth.

"Muuummmmmy! Sunny's being rude!" hollered Peter.

"Look who started it!" I hollered back. "Don't expect me to help you with your column addition."

"Muuummmmmy, Sunny says she's not going to help me with my coded addition — and she has to because she's good at it."

I'd been helping **the Twinzies** with their homework

since the beginning of term. It was kind of fun playing teachers and seeing their gappy-toothed grins when they got something right — but at that moment I wouldn't have helped them if they'd paid me!

"C.O.L.U.M.N." I spelled out in shouty mode. "Column addition not coded addition, and if you don't ever learn to get the name right, then you've got no chance!"

Peter started to wail.

"Right, enough!" shouted Mum. "Sunny, I expect a better attitude. Fix up!"

A vein bulged in Mum's neck as she spoke. I dared not say anything more. This wasn't the happy problem-solving image I'd dreamed of when I stepped into the kitchen that morning. I was doing the opposite of helping.

Once **the Twinzies** finished brushing their teeth upstairs and Peter had washed his face to clear up his tears (I knew this because Lena told me and showed me Peter's wet flannel to prove it), I dawdled by the kitchen door as Mum helped **the Twinzies** put their coats on in the hallway.

There was a small part of me that wanted Mum to help me with my coat like how she and Dad and Grandad Bobby used to when I was little. If I had two wishes in all the world (I wouldn't need to be granted three!) this is what I'd do. First, I'd wish to go back to a time when Grandad was well. Then I'd wish for the hands of time to stop so that we'd be caught with Grandad in that moment for ever. Suddenly an image of Grandad came into my head and I pictured him saying, **"Time and tide wait for no man. Life moves on — and we have to move along with it."** I stifled down the gulp rising in my throat.

"Are you walking with us to school this morning, Sunny?" asked Mum, interrupting my thoughts.

"No thanks," I said, "I'll follow behind." Really, I did want to go with them. I was sorry for shouting at **the Twinzies** and for Mum having to step in to sort us out, but I didn't want to say or do anything else to accidentally upset anyone.

"Okay, baby girl. I'll be looking back to keep an eye on you, so NO dawdling." Mum smiled.

Maybe she was okay after all? I decided it was probably best to let Mum look after me, and not me look after her. She did it so much better than I did. Plus, washing up

wasn't really my thing. The bubbles were making me
sneeze. I think I might be allergic to house chores.

I went through my usual routine on my way to school:
waving at Jakub at the Polski Sklep, Mrs Flowers the florist,
and Mr Chanda at Chanda's Groceries and Post Office.

"No letters today?" called Mr Chanda, waving and
smiling. He was standing next to the red pillar box outside
his shop. It was sparkling like a gem in the morning sun.

"Maybe tomorrow!" I smiled and waved back.

Arun and Charley were at the old willow tree, busy
showing each other something on their phones. I sighed
wearily to myself.

"Oh hi," chirped Charley when I was right up under
their noses.

They were so engrossed in whatever they were doing,
that if I hadn't turned up, I'm sure they'd have taken root
next to the tree. I was beginning to think that phones were
a very big and terrible distraction from the real world.
Though it's a distraction I wouldn't have minded having.

"Hi, everyone," I heard an excitable voice call from behind me. It was Evie. Her dad had dropped her off around the corner and she'd caught up with us at the tree. "I've had the **BEST** idea that **NO ONE** can say no to!"

We all looked at Evie with widened eyes. Was that a command or not? Sometimes it was hard to tell with Evie.

"What I mean is —" she said, more softly this time — "I've had the best idea that you'll definitely say yes to. Let's walk and talk."

We were all ears and walking legs. This sounded exciting.

"I told my parents about the charity day and they love the sound of it! They're really into raising money and doing stuff for other people... They say you can all come over on Friday to think about ideas and for a sleepover...and we can have dinner, but we'd have dinner first before we go to bed...and we can come up with ideas together to beat everyone else's stalls." It was as if Evie was speaking in one long sentence, racing away. Like she might forget an amazing detail if she stopped and took a breath.

Arun was the first person to disappoint her. "That

sounds like a great idea, Evie, but I'm really busy at the weekends with Star Makers and my audition piece for the School of Music and Dramatic Arts. I've got to show my parents that it's worth sending me there. They say it's too expensive, but if I can get a scholarship, that would solve everything. I've decided to look back into my past and choose a modern classic. I'm going to be Olaf from *Frozen*. Do you think I'll make a good snowman?"

Arun stuck his arms out horizontally, adjusted his head and wore a serene, yet goofy smile which made him look friendly, mischievous and kind all at the same time. I'd never thought about how to act as a snowman before. But there was no doubt, Arun would make a great Olaf. We all nodded.

"I can't make it on Friday either because it's Shannon's birthday and my family's going out for a meal," said Charley. "Maybe we can do another weekend?"

Evie's shoulders drooped. The excitement in her eyes was melting away.

"I should be able to make it," I said, trying to reverse the thaw. To be honest, we could easily have thought of ideas at school, or done the sleepover another time, but I didn't want to burst Evie's bubble.

Evie clapped her hands together in delight. "Oh, really, Sunny? Really? I guarantee, we'll have the best time. We'll brainstorm some ideas — as the grown-ups say — and then share them with Charley and Arun."

There was a moment's pause.

"Um…aren't we forgetting someone?" said Charley.

We were…

RILEY!!!

"Nah, I'm busy," said Riley.

Riley was a boy of few words when he wanted to be. We'd spotted him in the playground before school and disturbed his football game with Carey to ask him whether he wanted to come over to Evie's house on Friday as well. The interruption wasn't welcomed by Riley or Carey.

"Busy?" huffed Evie, waiting for more of an explanation. Another few seconds passed. "Well?"

"I'm washing my hair," he said, doing keepie-uppies

with the ball and avoiding any eye contact with us. We all looked at Riley's very short blond hair. A baboon probably has more hair on its bum that Riley has on his head. Well, probably not, but you know what I mean.

Carey laughed and Riley smirked. They'd both obviously read my mind.

Riley stopped doing his keepie-uppies and fist-bumped Carey; they looked very pleased with themselves.

Arun was now blowing so furiously out of his top lip at his fringe that I thought he might actually blow his hair completely off his head. Charley was chewing down on her bottom lip as if it was a piece of gum. Evie stood with her arms folded, getting redder and poutier by the second. I could almost see the thunder rolling in her eyes. The moment was...tense.

We were literally saved by the bell, as it rang out for the start of school.

"Well, Friday night it is then, Evie — just you and me.

Let's go!" I said, dragging my friends away. "We don't want to get a debit from Miss Fairweather for being late, do we?"

"Hmph," said Evie, looking back and glaring at Riley with steely eyes. "I guess not."

Teamwork was **NOT** making this dream work at all.

11

CHANGE

Fact of the Day: Sheku Kanneh-Mason is a very talented musician. He plays the cello and won the BBC Young Musician of the Year Award in 2016 when he was sixteen-years-old! His six siblings are also very talented musicians, playing instruments like the violin and piano.

I didn't have time to dwell on the charity day during school as we were too busy with our lessons — as well as doing test exercises to start preparing for our summer exams.

To "relieve any tension", Miss Fairweather took us to the school hall and got us to exercise to a soundtrack of

Black musicians, ranging from an American called Chubby Checker, who was famous for a dance called **the twist**, Jamaican singer Millie Small, who sang a song called "My Boy Lollipop", and finishing with songs from some British singers, including PinkPantheress and Craig David. Actually, it was fun!

On the way back from school, while Mum and **the Twinzies** carried on home, I stopped off to collect Mrs Turner's shopping order from Mr Chanda's (this was another one of Grandad's "little jobs" that I'd inherited). When I dropped them off, Mrs Turner gave me a lecture on how to carry groceries properly so that the tins didn't squash the fruit. Being charitable and kind was proving to be very hard, and quite tiring. Not so much the carrying of the bags but listening to one of Mrs Turner's lectures was not what ten-year-old me needed to be hearing every day. Clearly, Mrs Turner needed a new friend to talk to. I'd have to work on that as well.

When I got home, Auntie Sharon was in the kitchen. Auntie Sharon visiting on a Wednesday night immediately cheered me up. She was paying us a surprise visit.

Auntie Sharon was dressed as if she was passing through on her way to a nightclub, even though it was still only the afternoon. She was wearing an off-the-shoulder shimmery silver top, tight leather trousers and strappy silver heels. Her hair was short and black, with a silver fringe sweeping across her forehead like a dragon's tail. Mum, on the other hand, was dressed in a baggy, woollen jumper, clutching a steaming cup at her lips, like she'd just returned from a trip to the North Pole.

Auntie Sharon crunched down on a carrot. "Thought I'd drop in on my fam, check how you're all doing while your dad's away. Dennis, my driving instructor, dropped me off. To be honest, I think I make Dennis a bit nervous. He says my 'inappropriate footwear' is making the car jerk and mashing up his clutch. And he doesn't like me turning up the radio to full blast. But what else are you going to do when you're driving? All that concentration is a right old snooze-fest." Auntie Sharon began to cackle. "Honestly, Dennis is *so* funny, he breaks into a sweat any time he sees me walking up to his car. He says he's never met anyone like me before."

Mum raised her eyebrows above her mug and said nothing.

"How can you drive in trousers as tight as that?" I asked absent-mindedly as I looked Auntie Sharon up and down in her outfit. But I wasn't cute enough to get away with a comment like that, unlike **the Twinzies**. Mum spluttered into her cup.

"What's this, cheeky o'clock?" Auntie Sharon popped the last of the carrot into her mouth, walked over to me and gave me a hug, while crunching down my earhole. "You're inheriting your dad's skyscraper height and your mum's sarcastic sense of humour, I see."

Mum scowled at Auntie Sharon. Mum and Auntie Sharon bicker a lot, but they're always there for each other when it matters. At least Auntie Sharon was cheering the house up a bit — because, goodness knows, Mum certainly wasn't.

"Anyway, how's tricks? Tell your Auntie Sharon what's happening? How's that little boy with the movie star looks that dances up and down the place? I think he's sweet on you, you know."

I immediately felt my face fill up with a bucket of colour. "**NO!** Arun is my friend. My best friend, **ONLY!**"

Auntie Sharon frowned in disappointment.

"Besides, I think the only people Arun has his eyes on these days are Anna and Elsa," I said jokingly.

"NEVER!" cried Auntie Sharon, taking a seat and kissing her teeth, not realizing I was talking about fictional characters from the movie, *Frozen*. "Love rivals, eh? Gwarn, Arun, reeling them in already, is he?" Auntie Sharon let out a wry chuckle.

"Sharon! IN — A — PPROPRIATE!" bellowed Mum.

"My girl's growing up quick. You wait till she gets to high school, then you'll know the meaning of inappropriate," said Auntie Sharon.

Now, I was terrified!

At that moment, **the Twinzies** flew in from the garden, sparing me from further blushes.

"Auntie Sha Sha, you said you'd help us in the garden with raking the leaves and checking Grandad's roses for nits," said Lena.

The Twinzies were well-trained gardening soldiers. I'd forgotten that around this time of year we always checked for signs of fungal diseases on Grandad's plants, especially on the climbing rose, his favourite plant that he named after my Grandma Pepper. We always found it so funny when he said we were checking the plants for nits.

My Grandma Pepper's name, strangely enough, is not a nickname, it's her real name. Well, her full name is Pepperelda. And she's named after a plant, but not a rose.

"Jamaicans traditionally used the pepper elder herb along with a spice called pimento, by hanging them over an open fire to smoke meat and add flavour to it," Dad explained once.

"Oh, like they do on cookery shows?" I'd said, trying to sound intelligent.

"Yes, but it's not just fancy chefs on the TV who invented that kind of cookery, it's been around for centuries," said Dad, knowingly. "When your Grandma Pepper was born, your great-grandmother thought she would turn out to have a 'smoking hot' temperament, because of the way she used to holler and bawl when she wanted something. She used to scream till she went purple in the face allegedly — so your great-grandmother decided to call her Pepperelda — it seemed to fit perfectly."

"Harrumph!" said Mum. She always lets Dad tell stories about Grandma Pepper because everyone finds her so funny. But I don't think Mum finds her mum very funny at all. But to me, Grandma Pepper always sounded so very exciting and glamorous. I felt tingly at the thought of her. The butterflies danced and skipped in my tummy.

Although Grandma Pepper is my mum's and Auntie Sharon's mum, and Grandad Bobby's wife, she went to live in Jamaica years ago, when Mum and Auntie Sharon were teenagers — and then she moved to America. Grandad Bobby stayed in England to look after Mum and Auntie Sharon. He was meant to join her back in Jamaica when they got older, but then he stayed put after my cousin Dariuszkz was born, (you pronounce it Da-rye-us, but he now likes to be called "Daz") and then me and **the Twinzies**.

Grandma Pepper would call at Christmas, on our birthdays, and sometimes randomly in-between. She doesn't visit very often. She says the cold air isn't good for her throat. Grandma Pepper is a singer, so she needs warmth for her vocal cords to work properly. The last time she came to England was when **the Twinzies** were born. I don't really remember much about that; I was only four at the time. I just remember the beautiful smell of her perfume and her loud voice – and her buying us lots of gifts. But the best thing about Grandma Pepper is that she sends us American candy through the post. Yum!

Auntie Sharon's voice jolted me out of my Grandma Pepper candy thoughts.

"Get the tools ready for me, I'll be out in a minute, my twinzilicious Twinzies," cried Auntie Sharon, scrunching up their cheeks and chomping at them. "You're both so gorgeous, I could eat you for breakfast, lunch and dinner – and then do it all again the next day."

The Twinzies galloped happily back into the garden after being scrunched and munched by Auntie Sharon. She turned her attention back to me. "So, what's happening at school?"

I suddenly felt a bit twitchy – my neck hot and itchy. All I could think about was the secondary school open evenings coming up. I was excited to visit them, but I knew that I'd have to take something called non-verbal reasoning tests for some of the schools I was interested in, which was also making me feel sick with nerves. I'd already had to go through the grammar schools' exam in September — along with Evie — and that felt hard enough. The wriggly worms took over again.

I shrugged. "Nothing."

"NOTHING? NO — THING at all?" She kissed her teeth again. "Sounds like you need a hobby. How about karate? The class I go to on Thursday nights is working wonders." Auntie Sharon did a few hand movements and kicked one leg in the air like she was the Karate Kid. She had no business doing high kicks dressed like that, yet she still managed it.

It was hard to keep up with Auntie Sharon and the activities she'd taken up. Over the last few months, she'd been a whirlwind of activity. There were her driving lessons on Wednesdays, karate on Thursdays, and flower arranging on Fridays. It's like she was filling every minute that she wasn't working with something else to do.

Everyone seemed to have changed since we lost Grandad. Auntie Sharon was constantly on the go, Dad with his disappearing act, and Mum — goodness knows where she was at. It was all getting a bit much. The only people who seemed themselves were **the Twinzies**. We've had it, I thought, if the only normality was **the Twinzies** behaving like **the Twinzies**!

"Tell you what," said Auntie Sharon. "If Granny Cynthie and Grampie Clive can look after **the Twinzies**, let's have a girlie day Saturday after next, and you can tell your Auntie Sha Sha all about anything you want. Let's give your mum and dad some 'me' time — or should that be 'us' time?" Auntie Sharon cackled again, but then glanced over at Mum, smiling gently. Mum smiled back at her.

Auntie Sharon doesn't usually say or do anything without a **BIG BANG**. Her quiet whispers are a bit like the equivalent of a car alarm going off. So this exchange of looks and quiet smiles was all a bit on the down-low.

Did Mum really need "me time"? She looked like she needed things to distract her, rather than quiet time without us kids. I really was going to have to work out what was wrong with Mum, because I knew she was definitely **NOT** going to tell me herself. But at least I had my own "me time" with Auntie Sharon to look forward to.

12

NIBBLES

Person of the Day: In 2005, soldier Johnson Beharry received the Victoria Cross medal, the highest British military award. He risked his life twice to rescue members of his army unit, including driving over a mine to save their lives.

Suddenly, Friday came around. **EVIE DAY!**

My body seemed to be in a constant tickle-tournament with the worms and the butterflies since the start of Year Six, and that day was no exception. This was my first **EVER** sleepover.

The tickle started off in my chest, travelling down to

my belly, and into my legs. By the time school was over, even my toes felt a tickly tingle. I hadn't been to any friends' sleepovers before, not even at Charley's. Her house is always so busy, with all her sisters getting in the way! So, it was an extra thrill that this was my first.

"We'll keep it casual," said Evie to me at lunchtime. She then whipped out an A4 sheet of paper from her cardigan with a bullet-pointed list of what we'd do at hers.

This is what the piece of paper said:

SCHEDULE:

- **15:15 Dad picks us up**
- **15:30 Arrive through gates**
- **15:33 Mum says hello to Sunny at front door (Leave a few minutes for coats off and washing hands)**
- **15:40 Nibbles and chat**
- **16:05 Planning our charity ideas – including bric-a-brac hunt!**
- **17:00 Chatting about more stuff**

- 17:10 More planning for the charity day (and more nibbles)
- 18:00 DINNER!
- 19:00 Go up to my bedroom for extra chat, fun and change into our pyjamas. (If Sunny forgets to bring pyjamas, I'll lend her my best pyjamas!)
- 21:00 Lights out — but then torches under the covers for more chatting and lots more fun, without my parents knowing!
- UP ALL NIGHT!!!!!!!

"Well, this is very...detailed," I'd said. If this was Evie's idea of casual, I'd hate to see a more formal Evie. By "best pyjamas", she probably meant a ball gown and Cinderella slippers.

Anyway, I had remembered my pyjamas. This was *the* event of the year — how was I going to forget? Though, a little part of me was desperate to see Dad come back from his work trip that evening. I'd missed *him*, but how could I miss *out* on nibbles and staying up all night? This sounded like it was going to be fun, fun, fun — and very, very organized.

"Call or text over the weekend to let us know how the sleepover goes," said Arun, when we were all lining up to go home. "We can do a group call."

Charley nudged Arun with her elbow. His face flushed with embarrassment as he remembered that we couldn't have a group call without me having my own phone. "Sorry, Sunny," said Arun.

"Nah, don't worry," I smiled. "We can probably use Evie's phone for a group call later. Right, Evie?"

Evie frowned. "Well, I haven't written that into my schedule. So, we'll have to see."

Evie was taking this all very seriously. Part of me started to worry whether our sleepover was going to be fun or more like an army exercise that we should invite Miss Fairweather to.

As every child disappeared out of the classroom, Evie and I were the ones left behind, with our increasingly impatient teacher. "I can't bear tardiness," said Miss Fairweather tapping at her wrist. "Lateness never leads to greatness."

Evie looked down anxiously at her pink smart watch. Phase one of her million-point plan was going wrong already. Her dad should have been picking us up at 15:15 hours. It was now 15:25.

Evie's parents tended to drop her off in the mornings, just beyond the old willow tree, and when she wasn't in after-school club, they'd pick her up from the school gates in the afternoon. She lived a bit further away than the rest of us, but Evie still wanted to feel at least a little independence by walking part of the way to school without her parents in tow.

Evie's dad rushed through the school gates towards us. Well as **rush-y** as Evie's dad ever gets. Evie's dad is so cool, he makes a fridge look like an oven that's been roasting a turkey for two hours.

He floated in, dressed in a dark blue work suit, "looking sharp" as my Auntie Sharon might say. But he'd loosened his red tie and one button was undone at the top of his crisp white shirt.

"Hey, sorry I'm late," said Mr Evans. "On a Friday as well! Teachers work hard enough without me steaming in after hours. It's just the traffic, you know — everyone's rushing home."

(Auntie Sharon might also now say that Evie's dad was "as smooooth as hot chocolate".)

My eyes may have been playing tricks on me, but I think I noticed Miss Fairweather smile at his appreciation of her hard work. Her chest was starting to flush red; she put her hand to her throat, almost as if she was trying to hide it. "No problem at all. Evie and Sunshine have been waiting like angels," she said, sweetly. What happened to lateness not leading to greatness?!

"Well, we won't keep you any longer," sang Mr Evans, with a voice like pouring honey. "You have a good weekend, won't you, Miss Fairweather?"

The colour was moving into Miss Fairweather's face as she waved us off. This was great. Evie's dad had made Miss Fairweather speechless. Maybe while I was over at their house, I could persuade him to ditch his job as a hot-shot solicitor to become a teaching assistant at our school, specifically in Miss Fairweather's class. I'd never seen her so relaxed.

"Come on, you two, we have a strict schedule to keep," joked Mr Evans.

My face lit up. I was loving Evie's dad.

"Well, *you* may think it's funny dad, but *I* don't. You are **VERY**, **VERY** late," cried Evie.

"I know, sweetheart. There's no stopping traffic, except for when you're stuck in the middle of it." Evie's dad pressed the key fob to his Mercedes. The car looked as if it could fit half a dozen baby hippos inside and still have room for more. It was fancy, too!

I half expected the doors to open by themselves and for the car to drive us home, with Evie's dad sat in the back between us.

"Can we go home now, Dad? Mum will be waiting," said Evie, eagerly.

"Yes, ma'am! Chauffeur Dad at your service."

Evie and I climbed into the back of the car, and I sank

into the plush seats, feeling the coolness of leather tingle my fingertips. Or was the tingle caused by excitement? Or nerves? I think both.

The car set off, slipping into the after-school traffic, as sleek, slick and silent as a black panther into the night.

13

EVIE'S HOUSE

I hadn't realized that Evie lived so close to Strawberry Fields Park.

The park's real name isn't Strawberry Fields, it's actually called Beeches Valley Country Park. It has a massive activity area, man-made lake, farm, and acres of fields, making you feel like you've actually escaped into the proper countryside.

My dad calls it Strawberry Fields Park because apparently "Strawberry Fields" is a song from some old band called The Beatles, and for some reason Dad thinks it's incredibly funny. Because that's my dad for you. Full of jokes. Bad jokes that make you feel better.

"Why was six afraid of seven?" he asked when he'd FaceTimed us the night before. **The Twinzies** and me waited in anticipation for the terrible punchline. "Because seven *eight* nine!"

We all laughed. That was a pretty funny joke — for Dad!

"See, I'm as funny as Lenny Henry," he smiled.

"Who's Benny Hendry?" asked Peter.

"Never mind," said Dad, shaking his head and laughing.

Back in the here and now, Evie's dad drove straight past Strawberry Fields Park and down a narrow lane that I'd never noticed before. At the end of the lane, we turned left onto a narrower lane. At the end of this lane, we were met by big, black, iron gates. Evie's dad pressed a key fob and the gates opened, slowly and grandly. I did everything I could to stop my jaw from dropping to my knees and letting my mouth dribble all over the car seat. I never knew this secret place existed. I'd stepped into a wardrobe and found Narnia right here in my home town.

Each house we drove past had its own personality. One house was painted white, with pillars topped off with a lion's head on each. Another looked like a country cottage with criss-crossed windows, and rambling roses growing up the front wall. And one house had so many large windows, and a big glass door, that it was like driving past a hall of mirrors.

Evie's dad suddenly swung the car to the right and the tyres crunched against a gravelled driveway, pulling up next to a small electric car. The car hummed softly as the engine turned off, and I stepped out to witness magnificence.

If Evie's dad's car could hold six baby hippos, then surely Evie's house could provide a home for a whole zoo! It was *so* big.

The house had two sloping sides for a roof, which joined in the middle like an elf's hat. Two large square windows were upstairs, with one rectangular window in the middle, like the house's nose, filled with stained glass. And one of the bedrooms even had a balcony attached to it, which I'm sure would make Rapunzel proud to live there.

"Are you okay, Sunshine?" asked Mr Evans.

I broke into a radiant smile, feeling full of optimism.

That's a feeling I hadn't felt in a while.

"I'm just fine," I smiled.

Evie's dad smiled back at me. "Well, we're glad you're here. **Mi casa es su casa**: my house is your house."

My feet made a delicious crunching sound on the gravel as I walked up to the front door. This visit was going to be good. No, not good — **GREAT** — with a capital **G!**

14

EVIE'S MUM

Mrs Evans opened the large wooden front door. It was so big, I wondered if they'd used an entire tree to make it.

Evie pushed past me and her dad to give her mum a huge hug.

"Hey, munchy," laughed Mrs Evans. Her laugh was as light and as free as air. "Had a good day?"

"Yes!" said ~~munchy~~ Evie. "**THE BEST!** And it just keeps getting better!" Evie clapped her hands together like an overexcited seal and then stood aside, as if she was about to reveal **something incredible**. I almost stepped aside myself, so that I didn't get in the way of whatever was coming through. I couldn't wait to see it, whatever *it* was.

A surprise wasn't written down on Evie's schedule. But then, why would it be? Surprises don't announce they're coming!

"She's here," beamed Evie, pointing at me, like she'd just pulled off the ultimate magic trick and produced a whole person out of thin air. That's when I realized, *I* was the **something incredible**! What was so special about having me over? Evie must have had a million sleepovers before.

"Aw, so she is," said Mrs Evans, her hazel-green eyes dancing and sparkling like emeralds.

Evie's mum was dressed in a blue kaftan, covered in a pattern of cream flowers and brown birds. Fluffy blue open-toe slippers popped out from underneath, and her pink painted toenails stood out against the blue.

"A wah du yu?" said Evie's dad, changing his speech to Jamaican patois. "Are we going to entertain Sunshine on the doorstep?" Evie almost scowled, but swallowed it down, as she realized her dad was only joking. I wanted to tell Evie to take a chill pill, but I also didn't want to be rude. This was Evie's domain. Her show.

"Come on in," sang Mrs Evans. "You two want some juice?"

And just like that, I was in, settling down into a comfy blue sofa and sipping a glass of freshly squeezed orange juice in this large room, which seemed to be a living room, kitchen and dining room all rolled into one.

Delicious cooking smells mixed with the scent of flowers in the Evanses' back garden, carried in on the breeze. It was a warm October afternoon, and the kitchen doors stretched open, which made the outdoors feel like it was coming indoors. It was as if the garden was a wallpapered room of their house — decorated with some of the prettiest plants I'd ever seen.

I thought about Grandad Bobby and how he would have loved to see the bursts of colours from the orange, yellow and purple flowers. And then I thought about my Granny Cynthie. She'd be standing at those doors with a swatter, stopping any flies from getting into the house, like she was Venus or Serena Williams playing tennis at Wimbledon.

Evie and her dad both excused themselves and disappeared upstairs. "Back in a jiff," sang Evie as she skipped up the steps.

Even the Evanses' stairs are amazing. They're open at the back so that the stairs look like they're floating in mid-air.

I suddenly felt nervous without Evie in the room, but as I watched Evie's mum move around the kitchen so gracefully and easily, I began to relax. Looking at her, you wouldn't have thought that Mrs Evans had been so ill. She'd had cancer too, like my grandad, but she recovered. Evie told me that when her mum had chemotherapy, she lost most of her hair. But now her hair had grown back and she wore her dark brown curls in a ponytail.

"Your speech was so great last term," she told me as she cooked, popping things in and out of her TWO OVENS. "You spoke so eloquently about Jamaica, and the poem you wrote about your grandad was so moving. It made me weep."

"Thanks. I mean, thanks, Evie's mum...I mean, thank

you, Mrs Evans." I cussed myself inside-out for sounding like such a fool.

"No need for such formality here," smiled Mrs Evans. "I'm Claudette and Mr Evans is Carl."

"Okay, Mrs Evans," I said from behind my glass.

Evie's mum...Mrs Evans...Claudette smiled at me warmly.

I heard someone clear their throat and I turned to see Evie, sweeping down the floating stairs like an elegant...

...banana?

She'd changed out of her school uniform into a yellow jumpsuit. She'd also let down her hair, so that her long curls tumbled past her shoulders, while a yellow hairband pushed any curls up and out of her face. She was also wearing the cleanest white trainers you've ever seen, with a silver tick on the side and tied up with silver laces.

I'd been so focused on the sleepover at Evie's place that it didn't even enter my head to bring a change of ordinary clothing — I'd just brought my pyjamas. Now, in my plain green jumper, droopy pleated grey skirt, and long grey socks, I suddenly felt out of place.

I'm not sure how I was looking at Evie, but she must have guessed what I was thinking.

"Do you want to pick something out from my closet?" she asked. Closet? What was this, an American movie? It wasn't Evie's fault, but I suddenly felt really silly, which made me ratty. I thought I'd been so organized; I'd insisted that I'd pack all the things needed for the sleepover myself to prove how grown-up I was — and now I'd fallen at the first hurdle.

"No thank you, Evie," I said, through clenched teeth, feeling a sudden need to defend myself. "I have my own clothes at home. I just forgot to bring them."

The yellow banana shrugged and folded her arms. The air went a bit stale and stiff then, even though the doors to the garden were still wide open.

"Maybe later," I added, trying to make amends. Evie was only being kind.

Evie's dad appeared at the top of the stairs and jogged down them, with one hand in his pocket. I thought about my dad. He'd be pelting down the steps two at a time, descending as gracefully as a giraffe skating on ice, and the thought of that made me smile. Evie's dad smoothed down the collars of his cool white polo shirt, which he wore with blue jeans and brown slippers.

"Evie, I thought you wanted to look in the garage for ideas of what you could sell on your charity stall in case you decided on bric-a-brac. Your outfit will get covered in dust," he said.

Evie looked down at her yellow jumpsuit and shrugged, as if she couldn't understand what her dad was talking about — like her outfit was ready for the dustbin with the other banana peels. She glanced anxiously at her watch. "It's okay, Daddy, I don't want to change again. It's time for us to start digging!" This girl had a schedule to keep!

15

JIGSAW PUZZLE

Like everything else about Evie's house, their garage was **BIG**. It wasn't anything like my dad's messy man-cave shed. Everything here looked like it had a rightful place. Gardening equipment sat in one corner, tools were placed on hooks, and there were shelves filled with labelled boxes.

"Welcome to one of the best places to visit in the world," said Evie's dad. He had the same wide smile on his face as my dad has when he goes into his shed. Dad calls it his "happy place". I think Mr Evans's garage was his happy place, too.

We went over to a shelf of boxes and Evie's dad pulled a big box down and blew the dust off the lid, before removing it. We all peeked inside. "I had many a happy time working out all these games," said Mr Evans.

Evie and I started pulling smaller boxes of "these games" out of the bigger box. One lid had a train on it, one showed a garden scene, another a country cottage. There were lots of them. Jigsaw puzzles!

Evie looked puzzled — literally. "What are these for?" asked Evie.

"Well, why don't you have a stall selling jigsaw puzzles? People love them."

"You mean old people, Dad. This is the twenty-first century. You have to move with the times. Why would Year Four and Year Five want to buy dusty old puzzles?"

I must admit, Evie had a point.

Mr Evans looked a little disappointed. "Hmm, maybe you're right. Why don't I leave you to it? But stick to this area. NO touching any tools — and DON'T make a mess!" Evie's dad waggled a finger at us, pretending to tell us off.

Evie rolled her eyes. "**DAAAAD**, come on, I'm eleven now. You can trust me to look after Sunshine."

I was only a few months younger than Evie, not a

toddler! I did an invisible eye roll.

"I'll come check on you in a while. And, Sunshine, don't let Evie boss you around," said Carl.

I said nothing. I just smiled sweetly at Mr Evans, but inside I was giggling.

Carl chuckled and left us to it.

"We'll show Riley Edmunds what we can do!" declared Evie, rolling up the sleeves of her jumpsuit.

"What can we do to persuade him to join in?" I wondered aloud. Working out how to get Riley involved in the charity day might be the most puzzling jigsaw puzzle of all.

"Let's lock him in the garage until he begs for mercy," said Evie. I laughed, but Evie didn't even smile. "Tough love or tough luck — whichever," she said, shrugging her shoulders.

Was she being serious? Who knew with Evie.

We began rummaging through boxes to see what treasures we could find, determined that we'd have something to show for our efforts. We were searching for a good few minutes before we found a box of Evie's

dressing-up stuff. I pulled out a pair of giant yellow sunglasses, a pink tutu, orange feather boa, and some old plastic princess slippers. I put the tutu and feather boa over my school uniform, put on the sunglasses, and squeezed my feet — like one of Cinderella's stepsisters — into the slippers.

"Look, I do have something to wear after all! I *shall* go to the ball!" I announced, parading myself up and down the garage. (Well, it was more like a very painful hobble, in the too-small princess slippers.) Evie beamed, instantly relaxing. She put on a multicoloured frizzy wig, a red clown's nose, and a long pair of black velvet gloves that you see posh ladies wear when they're going somewhere fancy. She then put a massive fake diamond ring onto one of her fingers and started singing an old song from a

James Bond movie, called *Diamonds are Forever*, in a funny voice, throwing her gloved arms around in the air dramatically.

We both howled with laughter. I threw my head back because I was laughing so hard. I'd never seen Evie act so silly before, and that's when I noticed something.

"Hey, what's that?" I pointed to the top shelf.

"I don't know." Evie pulled up a stool and tried to stretch up to the object but couldn't reach.

"Here, you have a go!" commanded Evie, stepping off the stool. "You've got longer legs than me."

For once, the length of my legs did come in handy. I grabbed the handle jutting out from the shelf and carefully cradled the object in my arms, choking on the shower of dust that came with it.

I put the object down carefully on the floor and we hovered over it, with caution, as if we'd just found a meteorite.

But it wasn't a meteorite. It was a very old suitcase.

I wiped the case with the sleeve of my jumper to reveal a deep-brown papery leather.

"I wonder what's in it?" I asked.

"There's only one way to find out," said Evie, grappling with the case for a few moments, before giving up. "I can't open it! Where's the zip on this thing?"

"Here," I said. I took the case and pressed down on the two metal clasps. They made a satisfying click and the case opened. I smiled at Evie. "My grandad had a suitcase like this. He called it a 'grip'. I used to play with it when I was little and pretend I was going on my travels."

I opened the lid slowly and Evie and I both peered in to see what treasures lay inside.

"It's just some old clothes and other old bits," said Evie, her voice filled with disappointment.

"Ah, what have you found there?"

Evie and I nearly jumped out of our skins. We were so engrossed that we hadn't heard her dad come in. He walked over to us and bent down.

"My old grip," he said, softly. "I haven't looked at it in years."

Carefully, Mr Evans lifted the clothes — trousers and a jacket — out of the case and chuckled. "Our families made sure we looked stush when we came over to England from Jamaica, that's for sure. My grandmother gave me this beloved old suitcase, and I wore that suit on the plane over here as a boy." Mr Evans put the clothes carefully back in the case and took out some other things.

"And these are my wooden farmyard animals that my grandfather carved for me, before I left Jamaica," he continued. "I'd play with these toys non-stop. How I loved them so."

Mr Evans lined up the wooden animals — a goat, a horse, a chicken, and a dog — next to each other on the garage floor. "Woof!" he shouted, waggling the dog in Evie's direction. Evie let out a small yelp. We all started laughing.

"Oh, the fun I used to have!" Mr Evans's eyes grew distant as if he was travelling somewhere far away in his mind. "You know when I first started at school here in the eighties, no one in my class knew anything about me. Not just about me personally, but about the Commonwealth and its British subjects. Yet, I knew a lot about this country. All anyone could talk about was my funny accent and that

I was darker than everyone else. So, I did my best to fit in — to wear the same fashions as everyone else and to change my accent to sound like everyone else. But on the other hand, I missed Jamaica so much."

I remembered Evie telling me her dad was born in Jamaica, and that he'd come to live in England when he was little. Evie's mum was born in England; her grandfather is Jamaican and Trinidadian, and Evie's grandmother is white English. "A happy blend" is what Evie had called her family.

"Did they try to send *you* back to Jamaica?" I asked Mr Evans. I knew that some people from the Caribbean who'd come to England when they were little had been told to go back there, even though they didn't want to, and their families were here.

Mr Evans snapped himself back into the room. He seemed a little startled by my question. "You really know your stuff, Sunshine."

"No, not really," I said, feeling bad for asking. It had just come out — I didn't mean to be rude. It was none of my business. "Only, I hear my parents talk about it sometimes, that's all. They say it was unfair and it shouldn't have happened."

"Well, I've thankfully been okay. But, yes, some people were wrongly held in detention centres and threatened with deportation back to the countries where they were born. Some of these people came to Britain when they were very young on their parents' passports. They went to school here, had jobs here, paid their bills and taxes here, but because they were deemed not to have the right paperwork that proved their right to stay in this country, they were ungraciously told to go. Stripped of their dignity and everything they knew or owned."

Something about this whole kicking you out of somewhere where you've gone to school and worked your whole life sounded all wrong to me — but I didn't know what to say, so I just blabbered, "Well, I'm glad you got to stay."

Mr Evans smiled. "Why, thank you, Sunshine. I'm glad Evie has found a good friend in you."

"Dinner's ready!" Mrs Evans called from a distance.

"Come on," said Mr Evans. "Let's go eat! Claudette's cooked up a storm!"

Evie's mum had not only cooked up a storm, but a tornado and a blizzard too — the food was literally whirling before my eyes.

"Carl, come help me get this food on the table. You too, Evie. And don't forget what's in the warming drawer," called Mrs Evans.

I watched the Evanses in wide-eyed fascination — a blur of yellow, white, blues and browns — as they travelled back and forth from the kitchen to the dining table, placing plate after plate and bowl after bowl down. No wonder they have two ovens — and a warming drawer. Whatever one of those is.

"Wow!" I couldn't help blurt out as I approached the massive glass dining table. "Who else is coming over?"

"Forgive me, Sunshine, I think I may have gone a little overboard," said Claudette. "Evie's enthusiasm at having you over caught on — and because you were so brilliant talking about Jamaica at your celebration assembly last term, I thought we could celebrate the Caribbean."

"Yes, tonight we're going to have an eat-off, Caribbean *stylee*," said Carl, whipping two fingers across the air in a finger slap. "Trini versus J.A. And we all know which cuisine is going to win!" Carl grinned.

Claudette stood with one hand on her hip like my mum does. "Before you get too braggadocious, Carl, we'll let Sunshine be the judge of that. Good food doesn't just belong to one Caribbean island, as you well know."

"True talk, dat," agreed Carl, easily breaking from English into Jamaican patois. "We'll have to get Hannah-Jade up from London to help us eat it all!"

Hannah-Jade is Evie's older sister who's at university. I'd never met her, but there were lots of family pictures of Claudette, Carl, Hannah-Jade and Evie all around the house. Hannah-Jade is taller than her mum and Evie. She has curly hair too, but it's shorter than Evie's.

"Have you dined Trinidadian before, Sunshine?" asked Mrs Evans.

I shook my head. In fact, I don't think I'd ever met anyone from Trinidad and Tobago before. I made a mental note to write it down in my **Things and Places of Interest** notebook. Like I said, I do this every time I meet someone from a new country. I also put a yellow dot on my map of the world that hangs in my bedroom. My goal is for my map to be filled with sunshine yellow dots to remind me of all the new people I've met from around the world.

"Well, I'm delighted to introduce you. Come, sit and enjoy," beamed Claudette. We all took our seats, not for "snacks" as Evie had scheduled, but for the biggest banquet I'd ever seen.

Some of the foods on the table I recognized and some I didn't. I got to try:

Buljol made from salted cod fish mixed with onions, tomatoes, peppers, garlic, spring onions (Evie's mum called these scallions), and olive oil, with some avocado and bread on the side.

Chow – a kind of salad made with mangoes and pineapple, mixed with salt and pepper.

Roti – a kind of flatbread, which was served with curry duck.

Doubles – curried chickpeas on lightly fried bread with cucumber and mango chutney.

Macaroni pie – a lot like macaroni cheese in a pie!

Pelau – chicken, rice, peas and coconut milk. Evie's

dad said that sometimes this dish comes with pigs' tails! I'm so glad Evie's mum hadn't added any squiggly tails on that day.

Pholourie — spongy little balls made of chickpea flour with lots of spices, which we dipped into the mango chutney and tamarind sauce.

We also had the traditional Jamaican curry mutton served with white rice and pickled cucumber, and Evie's favourite — **jerk chicken**! It was all delicious. So delicious, that I couldn't resist a quick lick of my fingers. Mum would **NOT** have approved!

I thought of Charley as I devoured the meal and I imagined the size of her sky-blue eyes at the sight of all these different dishes. And then I nearly jumped out of my seat.

I'd suddenly had an idea for the charity stall!

Carl and Claudette leaned forward and Evie looked surprised.

"Is everything okay?" asked Claudette, probably thinking she'd given me tummy ache.

"Well, you've made all this delicious food, Mrs Evans…

I mean, Claudette...and I was thinking about how Charley and Arun would have really enjoyed the experience. So... how about a **FOODS OF THE WORLD** stand at the charity day?"

It was quiet for a moment. Maybe the Evanses were digesting the idea on top of their already full bellies.

Evie crinkled her nose. I braced myself for what was coming.

"I LOVE IT!" she cried, clapping her hands excitedly.

Well, I hadn't expected that answer.

"I think it's a wonderful idea too," Claudette laughed and then her face turned a little concerned. "But if you're talking about the world, there are so many dishes to choose from, and some recipes are quite complex, so you'll have to choose wisely."

"Well, that's true," said Carl, resting his hands under his chin. "But I love the enthusiasm. Now you have the initial idea, feel free to come back another day if you just want to kick back and relax for the rest of the evening. Bring Charley and Arun too, and the other boy...Ryan."

"It's Riley, Dad," said Evie, screwing up her face like it

had pained her to utter his name.
"I would rather bring a **T.Rex**
home; it would probably have
better manners."

Well, that stopped the
conversation dead. Deader than
an actual **T.Rex**.

"Um, thank you, Mr Evans. I mean...Carl," I said.
"That would be nice, but we've promised we'll share some
ideas with them over the phone."

Now that we'd been talking about Arun and Charley,
I really wanted to call them immediately. If I'd had my own
phone, I would have messaged them underneath the table
or something, but all I could do was wait for Evie to say we
could use hers.

Carl's smile was broad and bright. "Well, you're putting
me to shame," he confessed. "Do you both want to use my
study and look up some ideas on the internet?"

Evie's dad has a study!

"Oh no, Dad," said Evie. "We're going to my room.
I think we'll be more creative up there."

Before I had time to say anything, Evie pulled me out of my seat and up the stairs to her bedroom.

"I'll send up some ice cream in a while," shouted Claudette. With all the food in my belly, I already felt like Humpty Dumpty about to roll down a hill. But who can resist ice cream?

16

LAVENDER FIELD

We emerged from the stairs onto a wide, square landing.

Evie ran over to her bedroom door, flung it open, scampered across to her bed, flopped down onto her back, and stretched her arms and legs like a starfish. She was almost swallowed whole by a large pile of velvet, sparkly and silk cushions. I wondered if Evie had raided a pillow factory. There were also layers of throws, in different textures and shades of purple, draped across the bottom of the bed. Her room was a purple paradise, like Evie had been running through a lavender field and brought the field home with her.

I barely think about what colour my bedroom is. Beige?

Creamy brown? I'm always focused on the map of the world on my wall and the globe at my desk so I don't really notice the colour. But Evie's room was **AMAZING**.

"Oh, I feel so full and lazy. I don't know if I can be bothered to think about the charity day any more." She stretched her starfish arms and legs, like she'd been left floundering in the middle of the purple field. A starfish out of water.

Her bed did look really comfortable though, and the masses of food swooshing around in my belly was making me feel a little snoozy, too. Still, I really wanted to speak to Arun and Charley.

"Well okay, but we should at least message or video call Arun and Charley, and maybe even Riley, to let them know how we've been getting on."

Evie sat up, looking a little annoyed. "Why do you have to keep mentioning Riley? Do you have a crush on him or something?"

"Ugh, no!" I shouted, heat travelling at speed through my body and to my face. But then I realized the burning truth of it all. "Riley is part of our team, whether we like it or not. My grandad used to say '**where a goat goes, a kid follows**'."

"Huh?" said Evie.

"It means *we* have to convince Riley to take part by leading the way. Riley can't get the better of us."

Evie furrowed her eyebrows. "Whatever," she said, flopping back down.

"What's cooking?" asked Mr Evans, walking into the bedroom and interrupting the discussion. Even though Evie's dad is really cool, as the minutes went by, I could see that he was as embarrassing as my dad — well, to Evie anyway.

"Oh, Dad!" Evie rolled her eyes. "No one says 'what's cooking'?"

"Your face favour," said Carl, using his Jamaican patois again to say that Evie was being cheeky. And then he started singing some random song to Evie about being good-looking and what did she have cooking.

"**DAAAAD!**" Evie looked mortified. Carl just laughed.

"In all seriousness, any more ideas? Or maybe some traditional Trinidadian soursop ice cream will help?" Evie's dad whipped out two bowls from behind his back and grinned. I smiled back at him. Evie's dad may be a serious lawyer, but he's a lot of fun too.

We tucked into the ice cream. I'd never had it before. The sweet and sharp taste of the soursop fruit was like tasting a mixture of pineapple, banana and a sour apple all at once. And together with the creamy sweetness of condensed milk, it was lip-smackingly delicious.

"Yum! I'd love to make this with Mum for the charity day," said Evie.

Evie and I both looked at each other with widened eyes.

"YES!" we both cried at once. Evie jumped from her bed and we both ran round in a circle in excitement, still clutching our bowls.

Carl laughed. "I love the thinking, but ice cream in the middle of December might be a bit of a cold stretch too far! Hey, why don't I ask some of the patrons at the African Caribbean Centre for some of their best recipes?"

"Oh, yeh, you could," said Evie. She spotted the look of confusion on my face. "Dad helps out at the African

Caribbean Centre across town," she explained. "He does odd jobs like painting and fixing things. And he offers free legal advice too. Don't you, Dad?" Evie beamed with pride.

It's the only time I'd seen Carl's coolness slip. He seemed a little embarrassed by the compliment. "Well, you know, Jamaica is where I was born, so it will always be a part of me. As you so eloquently told us during your speech at the assembly last term, we are one people, so I feel compelled to help professionally and personally as much as I can. I promised my grandparents that I would work hard and achieve something. People from your grandad's generation helped me a lot when I was growing up, Sunshine. And now it's my time to give a little something back."

"Wow! That's amazing," I said. I was truly impressed — and Carl wasn't even braggy about how successful he'd become.

"Why don't you and your team come down to the African Caribbean Centre yourselves and get some ideas? Our patrons are very creative — and love a good fundraiser," said Carl.

"No thanks, Dad. If I want to spend time with old people, I've got you and Mum," replied Evie.

I threw my hand to my mouth.

"What a facety pickney!" laughed Carl. "I can see you're having a lot of fun, so I won't tell you off this time." He waggled his finger. "Think about that offer, though. The patrons might teach you young whippersnappers a thing or two."

"Oh, Dad, no one says whippersnappers!" Evie protested. "That's so not cool!"

Carl was creasing up with laughter now. "Well, I'd better get out of here before the temperature gets cooler than the ice cream from Evie's icy glares."

I grinned from ear to ear. Evie was wrong. Carl was one of the coolest people I'd ever met. He loved to joke around, like my dad and Grandad Bobby, and that made me feel nothing but happiness inside.

Carl took our empty ice cream bowls and left us to it. I'd been so busy shovelling the creamy deliciousness into my mouth while he was talking, that I hadn't realized I'd scraped the bowl clean.

"Wow! Your dad is great, Evie," I said.

"I know," said Evie. And I didn't even mind the boast. "Even though he tells the worst jokes *ever*."

"No, I think you'll find that my dad deserves that title." I smiled.

"**PILLOW FIGHT** to decide!" screamed Evie, as she started whacking me with one of her cushions. I leaped onto her bed, picked up another cushion and flung it at her head. Evie ducked and we both giggled. Then we started an all-out pillow war. Screeching. Laughing. Having fun. **SO. MUCH. FUN.**

"I'm going to win, because I'm the **OLDEST** and the **BEST**," screamed Evie whacking the pillow in my direction.

"Yes, I know...being **OLD** makes you **SLOW**!" I jumped across a couple of cushions like a grasshopper.

"That's unfair, daddy-long-legs! If you jump any higher, you'll sail up to the moon!" Evie was laughing. She didn't mean it, but Evie had raked up an old wound by talking about my legs being long and skinny. I suddenly tired of the game and stopped bouncing.

"Can we call Arun and Charley?" I held the pillow at

my side. If I'd had my own phone, I would have excused myself and gone to the bathroom to make the call without Evie being involved. And maybe to have a bit of a sulk about the daddy-long-legs joke.

"No, I'm having too much fun!" Evie bounced around like a kangaroo and then hit me hard on top of the head with a sparkly pillow.

"Ouch! That hurt!" I cried, swinging my pillow at her with a bit too much might.

And then Evie disappeared, right over the edge of the bed.

Thwack!

That's the sound I heard as she hit the floor.

I scrambled over the pile of cushions, pillows and throws, like an explorer trying to find the edge of a new land. I peered down over the precipice of the pillow mountain to see Evie lying in a crumpled heap below, reaching towards her ankle and yelping in pain.

Hurried footsteps approached from the stairs and burst into the room.

"She fell," I squeaked.

Carl kneeled down and checked Evie's ankle.

"Owwwww!" Evie's tears began to flow like a stream.

"Try and walk on it, honey," said her mum.

Carl helped Evie to her feet, holding her up as she attempted to walk. But it was like Evie was placing her foot down on a thousand tiny pins, as she wailed in pain.

"We'd best go to A&E and get her checked out," said Carl. And with that, he swooped Evie up into his arms and carried her down the stairs, out of the house, and over the crunchy gravel driveway to his car.

Evie was hurt, and it was all my fault. We'd been planning how to have the **BEST** charity-day-stall **EVER** and we'd been having fun. But now, I'd ruined everything.

17

CRUMBLING BISCUITS

Evie's mum called my house so that Mum could come and pick me up. She was going to head off to the hospital once I'd left.

Obviously, I wanted to go home anyway. It was all too embarrassing and shameful. And what if Evie hated me and started saying mean things to me all over again, like in Year Five?

The sleepover had started so well. I'd loved the ride over in Evie's dad's car — not that I'd ever go anywhere in it again.

And here I was, dumping another problem right on

Mum's head. I was supposed to be helping her, not making her life more miserable.

"Don't worry," Claudette told me, as if she'd read my mind. "It's not your fault."

It *was* my fault — I'd hit Evie too hard because she was getting on my nerves. That was the truth of it.

A squealing noise rang out, breaking through my thoughts. Claudette went across to the wall by the front door and pressed on something that looked like a little speaker. I could hear a muffled voice. "Yes, just drive up the lane, Number 14," said Claudette.

When Claudette opened the front door, to my surprise, there was Dad!

"Dad!" I ran to the door and straight into his arms.

"Hey, where's the fire?" he said, holding onto me and burying his head into mine.

"There hasn't been a fire, there's been a blazing inferno," I whimpered, raising my head and looking into Dad's eyes. He smiled and hugged me again.

"Thank you," Dad whispered to Claudette as we got in the car. "We'll check in later."

Dad screeched the car gears as we moved off the crackly, gravelly drive. "You okay, Sunny?"

I nodded but said nothing.

"Did you have a good time?"

I spluttered. Had Dad already forgotten what had happened to Evie?

"I mean, before Evie fell off the bed?" he added.

I shrugged. Really what I wanted to say was, "I was nervous at first, but then I had the best time! We ate Caribbean food. We talked. We laughed. We played. It was like our family, before we lost Grandad. Everything's different now and I hate it. I hate fighting with **the Twinzies**. I hate Mum being sad. I hate that you had to go away and leave us for work, please don't do it again. I hate that we have to grow up and grow old. I hate that I have to leave my school and go to high school. I hate that time keeps moving when I want it to stand still. I hate this. I hate it all. I want my family back. I want Grandad back."

Instead, I said, "It was fine, until Evie fell off the bed."

"Whew...swish house, eh?" said Dad, changing the subject.

Did Dad take nothing seriously?

Suddenly, I erupted. I couldn't stop the lava flowing out of my mouth. "Why are you and Mum being so strange?" I shouted. "Whispering to each other and then zipping up faster than a coat in winter whenever me or **the Twinzies** walk into the room? I thought you trusted me, but you don't. You say you want me to grow up, but then you don't want me to grow up, because you're always treating me like a baby. I want us to try and be normal and happy, for Grandad, that's what he would want. I thought things were getting a bit better, but now I'm confused. What's happening? I want to help make it better. Just like Grandad would've done."

Dad pulled the car over and parked. He took a minute before he dared to speak. "I forget sometimes how much you're growing up. But you're still my baby girl, and sometimes I guess we still try and protect you as much as possible. We've all been through so much."

I nodded at that. We had been through a lot.

"I'll level with you, there's been a lot going on, and I'm not always in a position to tell you all of our big people business," said Dad. "But it's only been three months since we lost your grandfather. And though we are trying to be strong for you — and the twins — sometimes it's really, really hard. And for your mother...losing her father... losing someone she has known for so long, who she loved for so long, is a struggle. A very big struggle."

"So, she feels like an orphan?"

"I guess you could put it that way," said Dad. "She still has her mother, of course. But—"

"But Grandma isn't here either."

Dad bowed his head and nodded.

"Why does Mum dislike Grandma Pepper so much?"

Dad sighed and raised his head to look at me. "Your grandma is a force of nature."

"Like a tornado."

Dad smiled. "Well, she can certainly draw you in with her strong personality. But she's also one of the liveliest and most generous people I've ever met. She lights up a room, just like your grandad did. But when she went back to Jamaica, and then America, she left a big gap that was very hard to fill."

"So, Mum has a gap that needs to be filled?" I muttered, cogs turning in my mind.

"Your mum probably misses Grandma more than she will ever say," said Dad.

"Okay," I said. "I understand."

Mum and Dad had been so concerned with making things better for **the Twinzies** and me that they'd forgotten about themselves, even though we could see them crumbling like biscuits in front of us. Sometimes I felt lonely and sad, but so did Mum and Dad, and Auntie Sharon. Even Mrs Turner. I realized that now.

Dad's revelation about Mum missing Grandma Pepper made me think. What if? What would life be like if Grandma Pepper was here? Maybe she'd help bring back some of the happiness and joy that we lost when we lost Grandad.

Dad reached down and squeezed my hand, and I squeezed his back.

"Is there anything else you want to tell me, now that we're having a serious grown-up chat?" I asked. "Don't forget, I'm going to high school soon — I can handle a bit of 'big people business'."

I knew full well that **big people business** usually meant **mind your own business**.

Dad chuckled. "Look, Mum could do with your help. I'm going to set you a mission to cheer her up. Can you do that for me?"

I nodded my head vigorously, though I wasn't sure how I was going to fulfil my mission. Mum was very good at looking after us, but I didn't really know where to start with looking after her. The more I'd tried recently, the more I'd seemed to fail.

I had to think hard. What could I do that was really special to help Mum? A bouquet from Mrs Flowers the florist? A box of chocolates from Chanda's Groceries, with my birthday money? I could even get Evie a box to say sorry that she got hurt.

Yes, that would be a good start.

18

NOR-FORK

Mum was sitting at the kitchen table when we got home. She'd put **the Twinzies** to bed and was nursing a steaming cup of lemon and ginger tea. I could smell the spicy ginger and zingy lemon as the steam from her cup snaked across the room to my nose.

Mum put her mug down and stood up as we came in. "It's okay, it's okay," she said. "Evie's mum called. Fortunately, she's been seen quite quickly. It's just a mild sprain. Evie's fine."

I was so relieved, I felt my legs wobble. I sat down at the table and Mum sat back down too, reaching out and holding my hand. "Don't worry, don't worry. Everything's going to be okay."

I connected with Mum's eyes. *Was* everything just fine? She glanced at Dad for a moment and then looked straight back at me. "Let me make you some hot chocolate."

Mum got up and hurried to the fridge to take out the milk, pouring it quickly into a mug. The milk slopped onto the counter and spilled like a waterfall onto the floor.

"Oh," she said. "Silly, silly me." Mum ground to a halt, like a toy robot whose batteries needed charging.

Dad rushed over to her. "Hey now, come on...no use in crying over spilled milk."

Mum looked up at Dad, right into his eyes and smiled, and then she buried her head in his chest. "I'm glad you're home," she whispered.

Watching them, I knew I needed to raise my game. I was glad that Dad was home too, but I could see I needed to make more of an effort. The mission to help Mum was on!

It was nice to settle down for lunch on Saturday afternoon knowing that Evie would be okay. Mum said I could call her, but I was too embarrassed to phone on the landline and for everyone to hear the conversation. And obviously I couldn't text her, so I'd just have to see how she was at school on Monday. I just wanted to enjoy having Dad back home. I'd missed him and his silly jokes while he was away.

But once **the Twinzies** and me had finished eating, Mum and Dad said they wanted to talk to us. They were sat next to each other, their hands clasped together on the table.

"Kids, we have something to tell you," said Dad. "I think you're all old enough to handle some big people business." Dad looked across at me and smiled gently.

"If Mum's having a baby, it's not sharing our room," said Peter.

Lena nodded.

Mum let go of Dad and started waving her hands in the air. "Uh-uh, definitely NO baby!" she yelped.

Dad cleared his throat. "No, not a baby, it's just work, you see—"

"If you haven't got a job any more, Daddy, you can have our piggy bank," said Lena.

Peter nodded.

What was happening? I wished **the Twinzies** would just let Dad speak.

"I've been made an offer that's very hard to refuse," said Dad. "It's a promotion opportunity at my accountancy firm."

"What does that mean?" whispered Peter to Lena.

"It means Daddy's very important now," Lena whispered back.

"Well, CONGRATULATIONS, Daddy," said Peter, like a game-show host about to announce that Dad had won the star prize. "Can we have our pudding now?"

Something in Dad's face told me that he hadn't finished sharing his news, and that pudding wouldn't be eaten for a while yet.

"You see, there's a slight twist in the tale. The firm is expanding and setting up a new office in Norfolk — and they'd like me to go there to help," said Dad.

"What is Nor-fork?" Peter asked.

"It's not so much a what, it's a where," replied Dad. "Norfolk is in the east of England. It's the most beautiful place. That's where I went to visit last week. It has gorgeous countryside and a wonderful coastline. We'll be able to go on lovely weekend walks and spend time there in the holidays."

"Oh," said Peter.

"Oh," said Lena.

"Can we have goats and cows?" asked Peter.

"Um, we're not moving there. I'll just be there for maybe six months or so — from Monday to Thursday. I'll be back on Friday evenings," said Dad.

Was this one of Dad's jokes? The worst joke **EVER**!

"You can't go!" I shouted.

"Sunny, this is a great opportunity for your father. For all of us." Mum was acting like a robot again, one that had been programmed to say those exact words.

My head was spinning. Mum just sat there with a blank look on her face. If she wasn't going to stop this ridiculousness then I had to.

"Well, Mum, you won't be able to visit for walks at

the weekend or holidays. You're afraid of spiders and I've heard that Norfolk has the **BIGGEST** spiders. As big as turkeys! What if Dad brings one home in his suitcase?" I blustered.

"Turkey spiders? That sounds awesome!" shouted Peter.

I glared at my little brother — **HARD**.

"Oh, Sunny, please don't," snapped Mum. "This is difficult enough as it is. It's an unmissable opportunity. You won't understand yet, but when you're older, it will make better sense."

There she went again, still treating me like a baby. And then I realized.

"That's what all the whispering has been about. You've been keeping secrets again!" I turned to Dad. "You can't go! Grandad's gone and now you're going. It's not fair! It's not fair!"

"Oh, Sunny, please understand," said Dad. "With this promotion, we can do so much. Maybe one day we can get a puppy or move house—"

Those words just filled me with terror. I never EVER

wanted to leave this house. Grandad wasn't physically here any more, but the memories of him were all around. His old chair in the living room and his bedroom, yes, but there was more. Everywhere in our house carried memories of my grandfather. From the garden where he grew his tomatoes, to the kitchen where he helped me with my homework, to the cupboard at the top of the stairs where he used to keep his rum. Every crevice and corner. Evie may have had the grandest-looking house in the world, but my house was grand too — full of the best memories and filled to the rooftop with love. Would my parents, one day, want to take this away from me too?

Ever since Grandad died, it felt like there was a hole in the roof of our house, where the rain kept getting in. And now that Dad would be away from home too, another roof tile had fallen off.

"I hate you!" I called, surprising even myself with my bite. "I'll never forgive you for this. Never!"

"Sunny!" shouted Mum.

I ran from the living room to my bedroom and didn't come out again for the rest of the evening.

OPERATION HELPING MUM

How could Dad even think of leaving us for most of the week?

There's no way Mum was okay with this — I could tell by the look on her face, her robotic voice, the way she'd been acting lately. And what about my open evening visits? We were all supposed to go together to look around the different schools — now Dad wouldn't even be a part of it. What about helping me study for my SATs? What about the charity day? What about **EVERYTHING**?

Before I went to bed that night, I spun my globe really hard in frustration. When the globe slowed down, it settled

on a country that swelled into an
elephant-sized blob before my eyes.

America.

And that's when a giant-sized
idea came to me. An idea that
could potentially help Mum —
and the whole family.

Would it work? It was the wildest thing I'd ever
thought of. I bit down on my lip in determination. I'd make
it work.

The next morning, I sprang into action for **Operation
Helping Mum**.

My thinking was, Mum had lost one parent, she didn't
need to lose two. And now that Dad would be working
away, it felt like we'd be losing — even though only
temporarily — another member of our family. Maybe
Grandma Pepper would be the missing tile to rebuild our
roof. If Grandma could "light up a room", then maybe she
was the switch that could spark Mum into happiness again.

Everyone else was busy lazing around after our Sunday breakfast of scrambled eggs — seasoned up with red peppers, onions and tomatoes — delicious fried plantain, and toasted hard dough bread on the side.

Dad seemed to be on a mission to cheer us up, seemingly by joking us to death.

"Hey, Sunny, what's a ghost's favourite fruit?"

I shrugged.

"**Boo**berries!"

The Twinzies fell about laughing over their breakfast. I did not.

"I need to get a new tickling stick for Sunny," said Dad.

I shrugged.

"How about your favourite ice cream for pudding, tonight?"

I re-shrugged. "I don't know. I don't think so."

"Come on, Sunny, even a ghost wouldn't turn down ice cream," said Peter. "The first thing I'd do if I was a ghost is get some ice cream."

"Well, that's silly, the ice cream would slip right through your fingers," said Lena.

"Well, then I'd-scream!" cried Peter. "Get it? A ghost is scary and put it together with ice cream. I'd scream! **ICE CREAM**? Do you get it, do you get it?"

Peter and Lena were laughing hysterically now. I couldn't be bothered to explain to Peter that if you needed to explain a joke, it officially made it unfunny.

If only life could have been as simple as one of **the Twinzies**' terrible jokes, I'd have been laughing all the way to happiness.

I turned down Dad's offer of more plantain — because if I heard another dreadful joke, I'd have screamed for real — and excused myself from the table. I was feeling twitchy. I had a job to do.

"Are you okay, Sunshine?" Mum asked, raising her eyebrows questioningly. Why was Mum always doing eyebrow gymnastics at me? I tried to be subtle, but ended up nodding my head so hard that it felt like it might fall off my shoulders.

"Do you want to pop out to the shops with **the Twinzies** and me to get some fresh air? Or maybe…talk…about last night?" Mum just wouldn't drop this bone.

"No! I mean, I think I might stay home and go through some more inspirational people for Black History Month, and then think up more ideas on what to do for our charity day stall. There's just **SO MUCH TO DO**!"

Did I sound natural or more like I was hiding a daring plot up my sleeve? I had my doubts on my natural acting abilities, but Mum bought it. She smiled, got her and **the Twinzies** ready and went out. Dad was getting his "Tony Time" reading the Sunday newspapers, not by sitting on the toilet, like he usually did, but he'd cosied himself down on the living-room sofa.

"Want to have a chat?" he asked.

"Maybe later, Dad. You've worked *really* hard all week, and you love reading your Sunday papers. Besides, I've decided to accept your decision. It's fine. You go to Norfolk; I can look after Mum."

Dad put his paper down, which isn't what I wanted him to do.

"Well, Sunny. You never cease to surprise me. You're wonderful, do you know that?"

"Sure, Dad," I said, desperate to get away. Also, Dad

had no idea of the surprise I had in store for him and Mum — for all of us.

Dad laughed. "Well, okay, if you insist, I might just read for a bit, but I saw this really great website on Black History Month the other day. Maybe we can look at it together later?"

"Yes, okay, Dad! Bye, Dad!" I was already making my way up the stairs, taking them two at a time. Dad would have us on that website for hours if I gave him half a chance.

I stole into Mum and Dad's bedroom and Operation Helping Mum began.

Taking out Mum's posh letter-writing set from her bedside drawer, I smiled to myself in satisfaction.

The golden sheets of paper were embossed with golden roses across the top and bottom. Swirls of golden vines swept down along the sides. The roses reminded me of the climbing rose that Grandad had named after Grandma Pepper. The writing set also had matching golden envelopes, along with a golden pen.

I disappeared into my room with the lifted goods, shut

the door quietly, gave the map of the world on my wall a quick thumbs-up, and sat down at my little desk. I spun my globe for luck and stopped it with one finger. I gasped at where it had landed — right in the middle of the United States, again. Yes! This was a good sign.

Taking the lid off the golden pen, I smoothed down the rose-covered paper and hovered the pen over it. My fingers tingled and trembled. I swallowed my fear, steadied my hand, and started to write.

Dear Grandma,

We need you to come home.

Grandad has gone and we are so sad and lonely without him.

Please come home, Grandma. Mum and Auntie Sharon especially need you. And maybe you could be a new best friend for Mrs Turner, our neighbour.

By the way, it's me, your granddaughter, Sunshine, writing this note.

Lots and lots of love,

Sunshine (But I've told you it's me already)

xxx xxx xxx

Maybe I overdid it with the kisses, but I wanted to convince Grandma Pepper how much we needed her back.

I didn't want to make any mistakes. No crossings-out. No smudged words. And I'd written in my best handwriting. Granny Cynthie says that Jamaicans take pride in their handwriting and I wanted to impress Grandma Pepper with mine. I needed her to come here — to England.

What's more, I desperately hoped she was all right. No one had been able to find her to let her know about losing Grandad, so she had missed his funeral. Mum and Dad and Auntie Sharon had tried so hard to track her down, but it was as if she'd disappeared into thin air. This letter just had to find her.

All I wanted at that moment was to see her face, to see what she looked like properly instead of just holding onto the memory of her sweet-smelling perfume. Mum didn't keep any photos of Grandma Pepper around the house. Auntie Sharon did at her place, and Grandad had kept a photo of them smiling together when they were younger on his bedside table. They made such a beautiful couple. My grandmother looked like a movie star.

Then I realized my mistake. How could I ask Grandma Pepper to come home when I didn't even know her address?

I needed Mum's address book, and I knew exactly where it was — sitting right behind her posh writing set in her bedside drawer! I face-palmed myself, disappointed at my lack of cunning. I would never grow up to be James Bond.

Avoiding any creaks on the landing, and sneaking back into Mum and Dad's bedroom, I took the address book. Back at my desk, I opened the book at "G" and my trembling finger filed down the page, searching for an address for Grandma. There was nothing there. Another mistake. I face-palmed myself again, almost giving myself a sore head. Of course! I needed to look under "M" for Mum. This time I hit the jackpot. To my surprise, I found what I was looking for, multiple times.

There were so many addresses with crossings out for Grandma Pepper. Exactly how many times had she moved home and travelled to different countries over the years?

Only two addresses remained uncrossed. One in Florida, America. The other in Clarendon, Jamaica. At which address would I find her? I didn't want to guess. A fifty-fifty chance didn't feel like fair odds. It was too important to risk it.

I couldn't ask my parents to photocopy the letter when they went into their offices, so there was nothing else for me to do but write another note. I summoned up the most patience I've ever managed in my life and copied the first letter word for word. Maybe the handwriting wasn't as nice in the second letter, but it would have to do.

I carefully folded the letters into their envelopes, wrote the addresses down in **BLOCK CAPITALS** so it was completely clear and the postal service wouldn't make a mistake and deliver them to the wrong addresses, and then sealed the envelopes with my spit. Mum says using spit to seal envelopes is common, and that you should use a bit of tap water, but there was no time to waste. Besides, Grandma and I are family — I'm sure she wouldn't have minded.

I kissed the letters for extra luck and placed them under my pillow. And then I moved them from underneath my pillow, just in case Mum decided to change my sheets, and placed them within the pages of my **Things and Places of Interest** notebook, before burying them underneath the box at the bottom of my wardrobe.

Was this the right thing to do? I swept away any creeping doubts quickly like a broom clearing cobwebs from a ceiling. Yes! This was the plan we needed to make our home happy again. It had to work. Mum needed mending.

I walked over to my globe and spun it again, more slowly this time, deliberately stopping it next to the North Atlantic Ocean. Fixing my eyes on America and then down to Jamaica, I bit my lip and imagined the letters as magic carpets, winging their way across land, sea and sky. I trembled at the thought of what new adventures were in store.

All I had to do now was post the letters — and wait.

20

OPERATION POSTBOX

Person of the Day: Doctor John Alcindor, known as the "Black doctor of Paddington", overcame prejudice from the Royal Army Medical Corp to become a World War I hero. A highly qualified and experienced doctor with his own practice, he volunteered for the British Red Cross, helping many wounded soldiers when they returned from war. Dr Alcindor was awarded the Red Cross Medal for his life—saving work.

Whether it was because of the tension in planning how I was going to get the letters to the post office without Mum knowing, or just the wind that had been howling through my dreams, by Monday morning I felt more exhausted than I'd done when I'd gone to bed.

"Are you okay, Sunny?" Mum asked for the fifty-millionth time since Friday night. She came over to me and put her hand against my forehead at breakfast. "Hmm... you don't feel like you've got a temperature, but I'll get the thermometer out just in case. I hope you're not coming down with something. Maybe you should stay off school today, and then we can catch up...talk. It's been a long weekend."

"**NO!** I mean, it was just the wind. It kept me awake most of the night. I'm fine. Honestly!" I said.

I was desperate to go to the post office in Chanda's Groceries after school to post the letters. I'd burst if I had to wait another day. This was urgent. I couldn't let Mum stop me. This was for her own good.

"Yes, the weather forecast says a storm's on its way. Only the tail end might catch us, but you can never be too careful. Storm Betty, or is it Catherine, or Doug? I can't remember which letter it begins with," muttered Mum, as she poured me a glass of water.

A little bell rang at the back of my head, warning me that there could be another storm brewing if Mum found out what I was up to... I pushed the feeling down into my stomach, along with the glass of water.

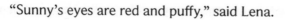

"Sunny's eyes are red and puffy," said Lena.

"Have you been crying as well as not sleeping?" asked Peter.

"No, but your eyes will be red and puffy through crying if you don't button it." I realize, considering I was in the middle of trying to be very kind and charitable to everyone else, that I wasn't doing the same with my brother and sister. It was the building pressure that was making me a bit of a meanie.

The Twinzies screwed up their faces but knew better than to say anything else. Not if they wanted me to help them with their homework.

"Maybe you should walk to school and back with us?"

said Mum, peering out of the window at the heavy-looking grey clouds.

"But I promised Mrs Turner that I'd pick up some shopping for her at Mr Chanda's." As I was always having to fetch and carry things for Mrs Turner these days, Mum backed off.

"Okay, I appreciate your enthusiasm for helping Mrs Turner. Just mind yourself and make sure you put your raincoat on if it starts pouring. I don't like the look of the weather."

I nodded and managed to swallow a piece of toast. I didn't like lying to Mum, but I repeated to myself over and over again that this was for her own good. And the bonus was, I had come up with the perfect excuse – thank you, Mrs Turner!

I was so distracted by Dad's bombshell job news, and my very brilliant plan for getting Grandma Pepper to come back to England, that I'd shoved thoughts about Evie's poorly foot to the back of my mind.

Mum had tried to convince me over the weekend that what had happened to Evie wasn't my fault. "Accidents happen," she'd said — but why did accidents always seem to happen around me? And then I started to re-worry about it.

Even though I knew that Evie's foot was sprained and nothing worse, anytime I did allow thoughts to creep in about Friday night, pangs of guilt shot through me. We hadn't managed to finish a plan for the charity day, and I was gutted that I'd missed out on the chance of sleeping in her purple paradise bed. It looked so comfortable and dreamy.

If Evie had blamed me for what happened, I hoped she'd have forgiven me by now. But, by the time I got to the playground on Monday morning, I didn't think there was any chance of that — and gossip was spreading faster than chickenpox.

Rumour had it that Evie and I got into another fight, worse than the one we had in Year Five, and this time Evie had **BROKEN** her leg.

What?! How did anyone even know about Friday

night? "Luckily" Charley and Arun filled me in on the details before school started. I'd missed them at the old willow tree because I was too busy at home — what with Mum's fussing, and packing the letters into my school bag in one-hundred-and-one different ways so that they wouldn't get crushed before I had a chance to post them after school.

"Maya Watkins called Evie at the weekend and Evie told her you were over on Friday night and that she'd hurt herself when you were both fighting, and then Evie had to go because her foot was hurting too much, and she couldn't say any more. And then Maya called Izzy James, and then Izzy called Dominika Kaminska, Dominika called—"

"Yes, I get it! I get it!" I said, cutting off Arun in full listing mode.

The only person that didn't get called it seemed was **ME**. Maybe that's because I **DIDN'T** have a mobile phone!

"It was a *pillow* fight! My mum said that Evie's mum said that Evie only sprained her foot." I heard myself gabbling. "She's fine...isn't she?" A huge wave of doubt swept over and drowned me.

"We only found out this morning," said Charley. "Maybe no one called us either because they know we're best friends with you. I'm sorry, Sunny."

"Seraphina says that due to the **severe break**, Evie will be off school for at least three months," said Arun. He shook his head sadly.

Huh?! My eyebrows hit the sky.

"If Evie's off for three months, what happens to our charity stall?" said Arun. "We'll have one less pair of hands and like, literally, legs. It really would just be you, me and Charley, because it's curtains for us if we're waiting for Riley." Arun swept his hands across his face very dramatically, as if he was closing a pair of curtains at a window. Arun was really taking acting and getting into drama school very seriously.

"Did you think of any ideas for the stall before Evie broke her leg?" asked Charley.

I ignored her question because this was getting silly. If made-up gossip was what having a mobile phone was all about then maybe I didn't need one after all. Or maybe I did, just to be able to defend myself against all these rotten rumours. "Evie did **NOT** break her leg, Charley!" I yelped. "You'll see how ridiculous this all is when she gets here."

But when we went into class, there was no sign of Evie.

"Good one, Sunny," whispered Riley on our way into the classroom. "If you break Charley's arm, Arun's nose, and then maybe your own leg, then I'll get to join Carey's group for the charity project instead."

"Oof!" I stomped to my seat because I didn't know what else to do.

Was this something else I now had to add to my list of worries? Where was Evie? Had she **ACTUALLY** broken her leg?

Miss Fairweather went through the register, calling Evie's name when she got to the letter E. After calling for Evie again, she looked up from her computer and then back down. As Miss Fairweather was about to mark Evie as absent, the classroom door swung open.

21

EVIE'S LEFT FOOT

Person of the Day: Despite being told she wouldn't fit in because of the colour of her skin, Julie Felix became Britain's first Black professional ballet dancer. She danced for the most famous ballet dancer in the world, Rudolf Nureyev, when she was a teenager, performed in a world-famous American ballet company, and danced for an American President and famous musicians. She even danced at an Olympic Games.

Gasps rippled like waves across the classroom as everyone stared.

It was Evie!

"Sorry I'm late, Miss. I hurt my foot!"

"So, I see," said Miss Fairweather. "I'm sure I can pull together a few exercises that will get you back on both feet in no time at all."

Evie smiled sweetly. Her left foot was wrapped in a bandage and she walked with a crutch. Evie hobbled to her seat, making a rat-a-tat-tat sound with the crutch as she moved. I felt so bad. And that's when I remembered that I hadn't even bought her the box of chocolates that I was going to as an apology. What a great friend I was!

Miss Fairweather got us to stay in our seats for our morning exercises so that Evie wouldn't feel left out. "Teams stick together!" she called, as we thrust our arms upwards as if we were boxing the sky and then twisted our waists from one side to the other.

We then moved into our charity groups to discuss ideas for the stalls. Our group went across to Evie's table to make it easier for her, but we kept getting interrupted by classmates asking Evie what had happened to her foot. It was like she had a magnet wrapped up in her bandages, pulling everyone in.

Evie giggled. "Oh no, Sunny and me weren't having a proper fight," she told Maya. "When we were coming up with our **SUPER AWESOME IDEA** for a charity stall — which, by the way, is going to beat everyone else's ideas — we were having a massively **BRILLIANT** pillow fight! And then I tumbled off my bed. It was all very dramatic. It's a good job I fell into a dance position, otherwise the damage would probably have been so much worse — that's what you can do when you're naturally graceful."

I couldn't help but smile. That was such an Evie thing to say. I was so relieved she was okay — and that the fall hadn't affected her over-the-top Evie self.

Once everyone had moved away from Evie, I bit my lip and came out and said what needed to be said. "I'm sorry I hit you so hard, Evie, and I'm so sorry you fell off the bed."

Evie looked at me as if she didn't know what I was talking about. "What do you mean, Sunny? Friday was the best Friday **EVER** — apart from my poorly foot of course. But even then, my parents bought me loads of treats at the weekend." Evie grinned wildly. "No hard feelings! And I thought about it afterwards. I shouldn't have called you daddy-long-legs, that was rude."

I smiled back at Evie, then wished again that I hadn't forgotten to buy her some chocolates. I'd been so caught up in my plans to bring Grandma Pepper home.

"So, what's this **SUPER AWESOME IDEA**?" scowled Riley, breaking up the happy moment, and sitting back in his seat with folded arms.

"Well..." said Evie, drawing out the suspense for as long as possible. "We — well, Sunny actually — thought about doing a world food stall. We just need to think about what foods to sell, because like there'll be literally thousands to choose from."

Riley scowled even more. "Well, that sounds like a half-baked idea if ever I heard one. Is that the best you've got?"

I wasn't sure whether Evie's head was going to explode at that moment, but her cheeks puffed up and she started going a bit purple in the face.

"Oh, Riley, can you just stop being negative for more than five seconds?" scolded Charley.

"Actually, Riley, I think you may have hit on a half-baked idea! How about **PUDDINGS OF THE WORLD**?" Arun swung his arm out in front of him very dramatically as he spoke. "We could bake a cake or sweets or biscuits. Basically, something that represents our heritage. I could speak to my parents for something Indian-inspired."

"Ooh yes, I could bring something Irish," said Charley.

I beamed. "**BRILLIANT**, Arun! I can bring something that's Jamaican. Evie, you could choose from Jamaica, Trinidad and Tobago and England."

Evie looked like the cat who'd drank a whole carton of cream. "My mum and me will come up with loads of ideas!"

"And what about you, Riley? Is your heritage English?" I asked.

The look on Riley's face was like he'd been made to eat a plate of cold, soggy cauliflower, covered in a ladle of custard. "Of course I'm English," he said, like that was obvious. "But NO. I think it's a rubbish idea. I think we could do something better."

"Like what, smarty-pants?" asked Evie. Her cheeks were puffing again.

"Like…like…let's do a **DUNK-A-TEACHER** stall!" Riley shouted so that the whole class could hear.

Everyone found this extremely funny, except Miss Fairweather.

"Yes, Riley, very good." She gestured for us all to calm down. "I've been known to take part in many an ice bucket challenge in my time, but not everyone is as hardy as me. I'd suggest this wouldn't be the best activity when we get to the middle of December, unless you want icicles for teachers."

Riley couldn't stop smirking at the thought. "We could dunk you in the school hall instead, Miss. It doesn't have to be outside."

"Well, it's nice to see such care and enthusiasm from you, Riley." Miss Fairweather pursed her lips. "Perhaps you can use this new-found fervour to serve your teammates with some more practical ideas for your charity stall?"

Riley shrugged and went back to folding his arms. "Charity day's going to be a load of old boring anyway," he muttered to himself.

I couldn't work out why Riley was being such a grump. I was trying to be patient, but I was beginning to agree with Evie — he was *really* starting to get on my nerves. I know Carey was his best mate, but was it so hard to be separated from him just this once? They were still in the same class, after all. But, then again, I'd have hated to be put into a different group to Charley and Arun — so maybe I should cut Riley some slack.

Another one of my biggest dreads about high school was being separated from Arun and Charley, if we ended up in different form classes or went to different schools. I wanted Arun to get into drama school — I really did — but the selfish part of me wanted him to stay with me. Being separated from school friends I've known for nearly all of my life felt too sad to even imagine. Maybe Riley was nervous and worried too? Thinking about that made me feel a bit softer towards him.

By the end of the morning, everyone had plans for their stalls.

Group One was going to have a drinks stall, including

home-made lemonade and hot chocolate "for a winter hug".

Group Two had decided on face-painting.

Group Three was going to do a basketball hoop shoot-out.

Group Four was going to do a bric-a-brac stall and sell old toys and games. Izzy James said that her grandad had loads of old jigsaw puzzles that he didn't use any more — and I felt shamefaced as I thought about Evie's dad's reaction when Evie and me pooh-poohed his puzzles.

Group Five had to go with their Plan B: a coconut shy and tombola. Miss Fairweather had discounted their Plan A of sawing their parents — and kids from Years Four and Five — in half, as part of a magic trick. Especially when Carey shouted out that he could bring the saw from his dad's toolbox.

And us, **Group Six**, we proudly said that we were going to present **PUDDINGS OF THE WORLD**. Riley grunted and muttered something rude under his breath.

Miss Fairweather didn't hear him. She was getting a bit carried away. She put her two arms together and swung them out like a bat, pretending to hit an invisible ball. "Home run! Strike! Hole-in-one!"

She then danced around in a little circle and kicked her foot out. "GOOOOOOOOOOOOOOOOOOOOOOOOOOOOOOOAAAALLLLLLLLLLLLLLLLLLLLLLLLLL!" she shouted. "But no resting on one's laurels! Let's get on with thinking about STRATEGY."

We were all confused, mainly because we didn't know what Miss Fairweather meant by "strategy". Also, what was a laurel and why couldn't we rest on one? And I can't even go there with her random sports moves.

"You've knocked the ball out of the park with your ideas, but how are you going to make your stalls fly? That's strategy!" Miss Fairweather jumped into the air and made a move as if she was shooting a ball into a basketball hoop. "How are you going to slam-dunk this thing into the stratosphere? What's your plan? What's your jam? What kind of puddings will you bake? How will you dress your stalls? How high will your hoop be? Any particular designs for your face-painting? **PLAN. PLAN. PLAN**. And don't forget, people, teamwork, will make your—"

"Dreams work!" we all chanted.

Miss Fairweather looked very pleased with herself and pumped her fist in the air.

I wasn't sure whether our team was going to make this dream work. On the way out to the playground at lunch, Riley gave me the dirtiest look. "Teacher's pet!" he whispered and then skulked off with Carey.

Riley looked like he'd happily slam-dunk me into Miss Fairweather's invisible hoop, given half the chance.

22

BAKE OFF!

** Bonus** Person of the Day: Ainsley Harriott is a famous chef. He was awarded an MBE in 2020 for his services to television broadcasting and making really tasty food. Ready, steady, cook!

"All I know is that our puddings have to be the best-tasting things **EVER** made if we're going to win this thing. So good that they could win Bake Off!" said Evie.

"Um, I don't think the charity day is supposed to be a competition," said Arun. "The stalls won't be marked — there aren't any judges."

"Yes, yes I know," said Evie, dismissively. "That's not the point. The reports that get written up on what we do will get sent to our new schools. We get to impress our new teachers before we even start high school."

Oof! It was hard enough impressing teachers at the school we were already at, let alone impressing teachers we hadn't even met yet.

Evie stretched down to rub at her ankle. I could tell by the scrunched-up look on her face that it probably hurt more than she was letting on. A pang of guilt stabbed at my insides, as the memory of her tumbling off the purple bed flashed before my eyes.

"We still have to decide exactly what to bake and how to dress our stall. But we'll make it **FANTASTIC**. Are you up for the challenge, Evie?" I said trying to distract her from her foot.

Evie straightened up and then readjusted her hairband. She had a calm look of determination on her face. "Challenge should be my middle name. I'm ready!"

"Are you sure you're okay with your poorly foot, though?" asked Charley.

"Oh, don't worry about me. It takes athletes half as long as ordinary people to recover from injury. I'll be ready to roll in no time at all." Evie beamed.

I laughed. "Evie, you really are something else."

"I know," she grinned.

"Always and for ever!" I called.

"Always and for ever!" came the response — and Evie shouted the loudest.

"What about Happy Face?" Evie gestured across the playground to where Riley was playing football.

"I don't know, we'll think of something." I gulped.

"Are you sure you don't *like* like Riley?" asked Evie, her eyes filled with suspicion. "You're trying awfully hard with him."

I was getting a bit fed up of this. I was *ten* and had more important things to do than think about boys. "For the last time, Evie, we need Riley to work *with* us — not against us. If he does, it'll make our lives a **WHOLE** lot easier." I tried to think of something sporting to say, just like Miss Fairweather, but I couldn't, so instead I said, "Teamwork makes—"

"Yes, we know," sighed Evie, as she rolled her eyes.

The question remained: how would we get Riley to play ball with the stall? I'd be going for my girls' day out with Auntie Sharon that Saturday, so maybe she'd give me some tips on how to get Riley to listen. Auntie Sharon was always telling me to come to her if I needed any "boy advice" — but I'm not quite sure she meant persuading boys to help you with a charity day cake stall. Still, it was probably worth a shot.

But before I tackled Riley, it was back to sorting out Mum. I had a very important letter to post after school.

23

THE LETTER

Grandad Bobby used to say, "a problem shared is a problem cut in half", or something like that, so I thought I'd share my plans for helping Mum with Charley and Arun on our way home from school.

The grey clouds that had threatened to burst earlier in the day had finally done just that when we came back in from lunch. We could barely hear Miss Fairweather over the sound of raindrops pelting against our classroom windows and rattling the panes.

I could only hope that Mum, in a mum-like panic, wouldn't gather me up with **the Twinzies** like a lost chick at the end of the school day.

But by the time school was over, the rain had stopped and she allowed me to walk with Arun and Charley, and then go on to Mr Chanda's to collect Mrs Turner's shopping. "As long as you're quick in getting home," she said.

I nodded my head and smiled sweetly, crossing my fingers behind my back in the hope that I wouldn't get found out for telling untruths. Once Grandma Pepper was back, no one would care about my tiny little fib.

I think Arun was trying to be sensitive about me not having a phone because, as we walked along, he'd randomly check in his pocket every other minute to make sure that his phone was still there, rather than taking it out — and then sigh with relief every time he realized he hadn't lost it. I decided to ignore this slightly weird distraction and focus on telling Arun and Charley all about Dad working away during the weekdays, how my mum was sad, and about my plan to get Grandma Pepper to come to England and cheer her up.

"Oh," said Charley. "I'm sorry your dad will be working away, but isn't your plan a bit...what would a grown-up say...elaborate?"

"Yes, risky," said Arun, pulling his hand out of his pocket and placing it on his chin. "I thought your mum didn't like your grandma?"

I did *not* like that my friends were raising so many ~~good~~ bad points about my plan. Yes, these things *had* crossed my mind briefly, but I *hadn't* wanted to think about them too hard. I had a job to do.

"And what happens when she gets the letter?" asked Charley.

"And what about if she actually comes to England? What then?" questioned Arun.

This felt like an interrogation. Too many questions that I didn't have the answers to. All I knew was that I had a fifty-fifty chance of reaching my grandmother, either in Jamaica or America, and I couldn't let the chance go to waste.

"Well, if she reads the letter and comes home, then the plan has worked. **OBVS**." I tried to sound triumphant. Why were my best friends trying to ruin any hope of bringing my family back together? Didn't they want me to be happy?

"It's all completely fine," I told them. "It's a perfect plan."

"Are you sure?" said Arun.

"I'm **SURE!**" I heard myself bark.

Charley and Arun frowned. They didn't seem quite as sure.

"Fine," said Arun.

"Fine," said Charley.

And suddenly we were all in an awkward huff.

"Right, I'll see you tomorrow. Fine." I waltzed away from my friends, leaving them at the willow tree. The tree shook its branches noisily as if it was upset with me too.

Why couldn't Charley and Arun understand how important this was for my family? How important bringing my grandmother home was for *me*? There was no room for doubt, no matter how much it was trying to eat away at my plan.

My bag suddenly felt heavier on my back. I'd brought my **Things and Places of Interest** notebook with me to keep the letters safe, but it wasn't the weight of the book dragging me down — it was the weight of my friends' words.

Why is life so complicated? There were too many things fighting to be number one worry in my head. The little worms were tangling again. Oof!

Still, I was going to do this and nothing and **NO ONE** was going to stop me.

I smiled to try and reassure myself, but then the smile fell right off my face when I walked into the post office and saw the line of customers waiting to be served. Who knew that post offices were so popular? Why didn't these people do post office stuff over the internet like people did with grocery or clothes shopping?

Mr Chanda must have spotted my face crumple like an old crisp packet as he came out from behind his counter. "What an earth is the matter, Sunshine?"

"I'm fine, Mr Chanda. I just needed to post some letters to my...to a relative."

Mr Chanda beamed. "See, I knew you wouldn't be able to resist sending a letter sooner or later. Give them to me and I'll sort it all out. You get off home."

"But I need to pay for the stamps and I don't want to push in. I don't know how much it costs to send a letter to...to somewhere faraway." I don't know why I was hiding this information from Mr Chanda — he'd find out all the details soon enough when I handed the letters over. But I was so desperate for this not to get back to my parents. It would ruin everything!

"Don't worry about that, we can settle up later," he smiled. Mr Chanda reached over to the nearest shelf and plucked something from it. "Here, would you like these rainbow sticky notes? They're not in perfect condition, but you look like you need cheering up and the colours are so bright." The packet was slightly ripped but the notes inside looked as good as new. "And you never know when a good sticky note will come in handy," smiled Mr Chanda.

I giggled. "Thank you." Only Mr Chanda could offer a gift as quirky and as colourful as that.

I reached into my bag and handed him the letters.

Mr Chanda looked at them closely. "Grandma Pepper," he whispered to himself and then looked up. A flicker of doubt swept quicky across his face, but then he smiled warmly. "Anything for Grandad Bobby and his granddaughter. "Let's not delay. These precious letters won't magic their way by themselves. That's what the postal service is for!"

And with that, the letters would soon be on their way.

24

PAINTED FACES

After I'd survived Mum questioning me on why it had taken so long to pick up Mrs Turner's shopping, and then me pleading with her not to "have a word with Mrs Turner so that you won't be taken advantage of", I went up to my bedroom, closed the door behind me and dived onto my bed.

Aside from posting the letters, the best part of the day had been hearing about everyone's ideas for the charity stalls. I smiled as I thought about what Riley had said about dunk-a-teacher and Carey sawing everyone in half, but I grimaced at the thought of falling out with Arun and Charley.

I needed to do something to help me chill.

I played a round of the **A-to-Z All-Around-the-World** game, and then suddenly, an idea came to me. Jumping up, I grabbed my school bag and took out the packet of colourful sticky notes that Mr Chanda had given to me. Sitting down at my desk, I opened my pencil case and started doodling little drawings. We'd all been named as groups one to six for the charity day, but we could make this more exciting, surely? I bit my lip in concentration and then, after half an hour, sat back and looked proudly at my work.

Group One with their home-made lemonade and hot chocolate stall had become **The Lemon Heads** and I drew a lemon with two little stick legs and booted feet, two stick arms, eyes, a nose and a mouth. I  also drew a little mug at the side with a big C on it and steam coming out of the top to represent the hot chocolate.

Group Two's face-painters became **The Painted Faces**. I drew three round faces and then used my red, orange, yellow, green, blue, indigo, and violet pens to draw rainbows across their cheeks.

Group Three were renamed **The Slam Dunkers**, and I drew a big basketball to fill the space on the sticky note.

Group Four's bric-a-brac stall, became **The Puzzlers** with a giant jigsaw puzzle-piece drawing.

And Group Five, with their coconut shy and tombola, became **The Cocobolas**. I drew a hairy-looking brown coconut, with arms, legs, a nose, a mouth and eyes, just like I did for **The Lemon Heads**.

My group became **The Pudding Crew**. I drew the hugest, most delicious-looking cake **EVER**, with a crown on its head to show that it was the King of Cakes. I could've eaten the sticky note it looked so good.

Even though I can't draw as well as my cousin Daz, I thought my little sketches looked more than decent.

I then got carried away, doing little notes for Arun and Charley first, and then for all my classmates.

I put a trophy on each, with stars around the trophy, and then wrote things like "**SUPERSTAR**" or "**YOU'RE THE BEST**" and their names at the bottom of each one.

After I'd finished messing around, I was going to rip up all the notes, but why waste paper? No way! Save the trees! And, besides, thinking and writing all the nice notes somehow made me feel better. I tucked the doodles into my notebook and placed it in my school bag. And then I thought about Charley and Arun again. They were only trying to help, because they care about me. I'd have to make it up to them, if they'd listen. After all, I *hadn't* listened to them. Why was life so difficult?!

25

THE OLD WILLOW TREE

Person of the Day: Lenny Henry acts, writes, sings and makes people laugh. He is also very kind and co–founded Comic Relief, a charity which raises LOTS and LOTS of money for good causes.
He won a big TV talent show called New Faces, a bit like Britain's Got Talent, when he was sixteen-years-old.

The next morning, on the way to school, I wondered whether Charley and Arun had spent the evening texting each other behind my back about what a terrible friend

I was. We were all supposed to go to an open evening at one of the secondary schools later on — what if they wanted to walk around it without me?

I was so distracted by my thoughts that I only just remembered to wave to Jakub, Mrs Flowers and Mr Chanda.

"I've posted the letters. They're on their way! You can always trust the wonders of the modern postal service," called Mr Chanda.

That news cheered me up a bit. "Thank you, Mr Chanda!"

I doubted that Arun and Charley would wait for me by the old willow tree. Why would they after I'd barked at them over my plans to bring Grandma Pepper home? What good was it being kind to others, if I was a complete **rudey** to my friends? I held my head down as I approached the tree.

When I looked back up again through the branches, I glimpsed a bob of bright-red hair next to a mop of jet-black hair — and someone blowing out of their top lip to keep their fringe out of their eyes. Arun and Charley had waited for me!

They may have had their faces buried in their phones, but it didn't matter (much). It was hard for me to swallow my smile.

"I thought you two would be long gone," I said, playing it cool. They both looked up from their phones.

"Well...you know," said Arun, glancing down again and kicking his foot at an invisible stone on the pavement. "Always and for ever, and all that."

"Yes, for ever and ever. Amen," said Charley, smiling at me through warm eyes.

We didn't say much else on our way to school. As we've known each other since nursery, we didn't need to — and I didn't mention the letters again.

We had maths and English in the morning. After lunch, we were going to break into our charity groups to discuss our strategies for the stalls. That reminded me of the sticky-note drawings in my bag. I suddenly felt really shy about my classmates seeing them. Maybe they'd think they were silly. Not a Year Six kind of thing to do? But something inside of me still wanted to share them. So, after our lunch sitting, I suddenly grasped at my tummy.

"Are you, okay, Sunny?" asked Charley, looking concerned, and about to diagnose me with an illness straight out of one of her mum's medical books.

"Oh, I think my orange juice might have been a bit off. Tummy troubles," I whispered, scrunching up my face. "I think I'll just pop to the loo."

Charley, Arun and Evie gave me a sympathetic look and headed (Evie hobbled) to the playground for the rest of lunch, while I went towards the toilets, making a swift detour into our classroom, swiping my bag off my peg as I went in.

I hurriedly took the sticky notes out of my bag and started putting all the ones with trophies and names onto each of my classmates' seats.

And that's when the classroom door opened.

"Sunny, what are you doing in here?" It was Miss Peach; I'd been caught red sticky-note handed!

I quickly threw my hands behind my back, but it was too late.

Miss Peach walked over to me with one hand held out. She didn't look pleased. I placed the wad of notes into her palm.

She looked at them closely. "What are these, Sunny?"

I confessed all to Miss Peach and told her that, to jazz up the charity day, I'd wanted to surprise everyone with the little notes by giving our groups names.

"I'm sorry, Miss Peach, am I in trouble?"

Miss Peach looked up at me. It was like her usually soft, brown eyes were blazing into my soul. "Absolutely...not!" she cried. "This is a brilliant idea, Sunshine. I'll help you!"

We worked quickly. I carried on putting notes onto chairs and Miss Peach put the ones with the new group names on the wall behind Miss Fairweather's desk.

"Can we keep this as a surprise, Miss?" I asked, when we'd finished. ~~Part of me~~ A lot of me now felt *even more* embarrassed and worried by my silly, little notes. I didn't want my classmates to know it was me.

"A ghost writer...what fun!" Miss Peach winked. "I won't tell a soul."

Miss Peach is the best!

"Hey, there's a sticky note on my seat with my name on it; it's got a trophy and stars drawn all around it," said Marcus. "And it says I'm a superstar."

"And me!"

"And me!"

There were lots of "and me"s echoing through the class.

"And what's this?" asked Miss Fairweather, as she looked at the notes on the wall.

"Did you see who did it?" asked Charley. "I mean when you went to the loo?" Charley whispered "the loo" bit so that she didn't embarrass me about my "tummy troubles".

"Not a thing," I whispered back, still holding my tummy, and making funny facial expressions.

I'd even hurriedly written a note for myself, so no one would suspect it was me.

"Well, well, well...it looks like we have a phantom writer and artist in the school. I love the sporting spirit!" sang Miss Fairweather. "Let's hear it for our new groups — The Lemon Heads, The Painted Faces, The Puzzlers, The

Slam Dunkers, The Cocobolas — and The Pudding Crew!"

If Miss Fairweather had pom-poms stashed away in her drawer, I'm sure she would have whipped them out, jumped into the air shaking them, and then gone straight into splits on the floor. She was as excited as a cheerleader.

When all the fuss had died down, the Pudding Crew went over to work at Evie's desk to save her from hobbling around.

"I don't even like puddings," Riley grumped, as we settled ourselves.

After everyone had been so enthusiastic about the sticky notes, this news brought me crashing back down to earth with a wallop.

Evie pretended to yawn. "**BOORRR-ING.** Everyone likes puddings. Cakes? Biscuits? You must like something!"

Riley shook his head firmly. "Nope."

This whole afternoon had the potential to be as explosive as a firework and fish pie milkshake!

"Why don't we go through some ideas. You never know, you might find you like *something*, Riley," I said, desperately trying to keep the peace.

"Well, me and my parents went through a load of ideas last night and I think I want to make my favourite pudding called gajar ka halwa. They're little pots made with carrots and a lot of yumminess," said Arun, rubbing his tummy and licking his lips, like he couldn't wait.

Charley grinned. "Ooh, yes, that sounds great, Arun. I'm still deciding between Irish apple cake, Irish shortbread, or Irish oat cookies. Just know, whatever I make it will definitely be Irish."

"My parents say it will be too cold and impractical to make soursop ice cream, which is really popular in Trinidad and Tobago, so I'll probably go with Trinidadian sponge cake or coconut fudge," explained Evie.

Riley rolled his eyes. "Well, none of those are going to be as nice as angel cake, or chocolate cake, or jam roly-poly, or Victoria sponge cake."

"**Ex-CUUUSSE** me, Riley. But for someone who doesn't like puddings, you seem to know quite a lot of them," scoffed Evie.

With that, Riley went into a huff again.

"Well, why don't you make one of those, Riley?" I said.

"They're all lovely. What about the Victoria sponge or chocolate cake? Everyone likes a bit of jam and cream or chocolate, don't they?"

Arun and Charley nodded encouragingly. Meanwhile, Evie stuck her nose in the air and Riley folded his arms.

"Nah, I'll pass," he snorted.

"What about you, Sunny?" asked Charley, deciding to abandon any hope of persuading Riley.

"Well...um..." To be honest, because of all the fussing over the letter to Grandma Pepper and then doodling the sticky notes, I hadn't given my charity day pudding a minute's thought. Then I remembered who could save me.

"My Granny Cynthie makes amazing Jamaican rum cakes!" I chimed. "I'll probably make one of those, but without the rum."

We all grinned, except Riley. A tickling stick with a million feathers on the end of it probably couldn't get him to crack even the hint of a smile.

After a few more minutes of Riley huffing, Evie puffing, and Charley, Arun and me desperately trying to keep us all on track, we made our final-ish list:

Arun — Gajar ka halwa sweet carrot pudding

Charley — Irish apple cake, shortbread or oat cookies

Evie — Trinidadian sponge cake and / or coconut fudge

Sunshine — Jamaican not-any-rum-in-it cake

Riley — Victoria sponge or chocolate cake?????

Looking at the list and all the question marks after Riley's entry, something really started to trouble me. What was Riley's problem? We'd managed to get along for years without bothering each other, and now he seemed to really have it in for me.

Oof! Sad times.

26

OPEN EVENING

That night, when Mum, Dad, **the Twinzies** and me headed to the open evening at Greenhill Academy, my feelings changed to a mixture of excitement and terror. The worms and the butterflies were having an all-out fight to come out on top, and I wasn't sure which was winning.

Mum made me shower, redo my hair, and put on a dress, as if I was going to meet the King. At least Dad's working away from home wouldn't begin until after half-term, at the start of November, so he could make it.

We met up with Charley and her mum, and Arun and his parents outside Greenhill Academy. My dad had been to the school yonks ago when he was a kid, but it was called Greenhill High School then. The original school had been opened in the 1930s, Dad told me. Not because he'd gone there then — even he's not that old! But it had changed a lot since, with a new extension built when the school became an academy ten years ago.

"Whew, this is grand!" said Dad and then he made his voice sound like an old man. "And there's no cart and horses in the playground, like when I were a lad."

All the grown-ups found this joke very funny. I wished Evie was here. I'd told her that my dad's jokes were worse than her dad's. But Evie and her family had to make a special arrangement to see the school another time, due to her poorly foot.

I gulped and linked arms with Arun and Charley as we walked up to the main entrance. The automatic glass doors parted slowly and smoothly, and we walked in.

Dad was right, the school *was* grand.

The main reception area was to the right and to the left sat a huge trophy cabinet. The trophies glistened proudly from their glass case, boasting of the school's achievements. As we craned our heads upwards, we saw a stream of people busily walking in and out of classrooms. This school had two floors. Beeches Primary just has one flat pancake layer, so this would be a big step up — literally.

More and more families piled in behind us and then we were whisked into a hall for a talk from the head teacher, Mr Baker. As we sat down, Dad reached into his man bag and pulled out a spreadsheet. It was around a fifty-point list that had categories including ambition, attainment and values. He began jotting notes down and ticking things off in the columns with different coloured marker pens. Dad looked very satisfied by the end of Mr Baker's talk. Charley's mum and Arun's dad asked if they could get photocopies of the spreadsheet. Charley, Arun and I rolled our eyes.

Then we were all herded out of the hall because some of the Year Eights and Nines were going to give families a tour of the school, so we were broken into smaller groups. Thankfully, Charley's, Arun's and my family stayed together.

I recognized one of the tour guides immediately. Katie Matthews had gone to Beeches Primary, but I didn't recognize the other girl.

"Haven't you three grown up? Especially you, Sunshine. You're so tall!" said Katie, like she was an adult and not thirteen.

Arun, Charley and me all looked at each other, our mouths wide open. We were so shocked that Katie even knew who we were; she didn't look in our direction once at primary school. We just nodded, and said nothing, like we'd suddenly lost our voices.

"Aren't you three funny?" said Katie, who then turned to speak to our parents.

"I'm Katie and this is Bella," she said. "We'll be taking you on a tour of our school. If you have any questions, please don't be afraid to ask." All our parents smiled, really impressed at their good manners — and Dad got out his spreadsheet and ticked something else off.

Then Peter Twinzie tugged at Dad's arm and whispered something into his ear.

"Ah, could you point us in the direction of the facilities, please, Katie and Bella?" asked Dad. Neither Katie nor Bella seemed to know what Dad was talking about, even though they said we could ask any question we liked. I mean, to be fair, who says facilities when they mean the toilet?

Once Katie and Bella had cottoned on to the bathroom situation, they were like air traffic controllers pointing in the direction of "the facilities".

Charley started blinking rapidly at Arun and me. Charley can't wink with one eye; instead, she blinks with two. I guess it's a bit like someone who can't whistle with two fingers or pop the inside of their mouth when singing "Pop Goes the Weasel". Anyway, both Arun and me were wondering why Charley was **blink winking**.

"I think I might pop to the loos too," she said. And then we realized what she was up to. Charley was on a mission to make sure the toilets were up to her standards, just in case anyone decided to flush her head down one in Year Seven.

I winked back. "Okay, Charley, see you in a min."

By the time Dad, Peter and Charley had returned to reception, Katie and Bella had abandoned us for another group. "Got to keep to a tight schedule," said Katie.

Mum nodded her head approvingly at their timekeeping and said that we'd wait for the next tour guides.

We ended up being shown round by a really tall boy called Troy and a shorter boy called Malik, who were actually really nice, too.

"I barely recognize the place," said Dad. He was acting like we'd won a ticket to Willy Wonka's chocolate factory. His mouth was wide open on our way round the classrooms, marvelling at all the changes. As long as he didn't start licking the walls or eating bits of furniture, like we really were in the chocolate factory, we'd be fine.

We were shown the sports hall and art block, the dance studio — which Arun loved — and the science block. We even got to put on goggles and use the Bunsen burner in the chemistry class. And in maths, we sat down to do a little quiz on a computer game maths app, which was really fun. Charley, Arun and me had to do ours on our own, but one of the school's students helped **the Twinzies** —

and they ended up winning a calculator! I know **the Twinzies** were just six years old, but three against one wasn't fair odds! I soon changed my tune when **the Twinzies** gave me the calculator, though. "You need this more than we do," said Lena smiling a gap-toothed smile at me.

"Yes, we're maths geniuses," grinned Peter. "We don't need a calculator."

I didn't know whether to smile or scowl — **the Twinzies** are something else. Mostly, very, very cute.

By the time we got to the end of the tour, Charley, Arun and me realized something. We really liked the school — and Charley gave the toilets seven out of ten.

"I think there's room for loo improvement," said Charley. "But I really like it here."

We still had another few schools to visit, but I really liked it, too. "What about a strategy for cleaner toilets? 'We want clean loos for number ones and number twos!' Miss Fairweather will love it!" I joked.

We giggled, but then Arun suddenly looked worried.

"If I don't get into the School of Music and Dramatic

Arts, I think I'd like to go here. Oh...I'm so nervous about my audition tomorrow and what my parents will think of the school. I really, *really* want to go to drama school. Can you tell me to break a leg, please?"

"Why would we want you to break your leg?" asked Charley.

"It's for good luck," I said. "If you're an actor."

"Oh," said Charley.

"Break a leg!" we both said unanimously.

When I got home, I went to my bedroom and took out my **No Worries** book from the box in my wardrobe and wrote down what I thought.

Yes, Greenhill Academy was big and a bit scary, but the teachers were nice, and I liked the classrooms. The geography teacher had a huge map of the world on one of her walls — just like my bedroom.

Maybe secondary school wouldn't be so bad after all? Especially if my friends from Beeches Primary were there with me. Even if they weren't, maybe I'd make new friends like Troy and Malik or Katie and Bella. This would be a new adventure, that's how Grandad Bobby would tell me to see it, and just thinking about that made me feel better.

27

EVERY MICKLE MAKES A MUCKLE

By the time we got to Friday and broke up for half-term, I let out a huge sigh of relief.

We'd done a few more visits to other high schools in that week — including Beeches Grammar School, which I'd sat a test for in September with Evie. It was so posh, and I couldn't help but wonder, even if by a miracle I got in, would I really like it if none of my friends were there? Well, except Evie, she'd been practising for grammar school since for ever, so no doubt she'd get in. Though, even Evie seemed to be really nervous on the actual test day. Not the confident Evie I knew so well. She was more of a rabbit caught in a very bright headlight by the end of the test.

To keep myself distracted, I'd been writing a few sticky notes every day for my classmates and dotting them around on their seats and desks, whenever I sneakily could. I'd even drawn one of Riley in his football kit with a trophy in his hand. He scowled as he looked at it, and then scrunched it up and put it in his pocket. **RUDE!!!**

Anyway, Arun was on cloud nine. He was buzzing after his audition at the School of Music and Dramatic Arts.

"How did it go?" I'd asked.

"They said I 'injected great warmth and creativity into the role'," said Arun.

"A warm snowman is pretty good, right?" asked Charley.

"Well, no, but yes, in this case, I hope so," smiled Arun. "My parents seemed impressed with the school, too. But they're still a little unsure, even though the head teacher explained that there'll be a balance between the schoolwork and the music and drama. I hope I've done enough to get the scholarship."

"I bet you have," I said, putting an encouraging arm around his shoulder. "I just know it!"

Year Six was already proving to be so tiring, frightening and exciting all at the same time — and it was still only October.

At least I had my visit to Auntie Sharon's for our girls' day out to look forward to. There's nothing like spending time with Auntie Sharon to chase away your worries.

"Ready to go soon?" Dad had asked on Saturday morning. I'd never been more ready. It's a shame the same couldn't be said for Auntie Sharon.

After about ten minutes of us knocking and ringing the doorbell, Auntie Sharon flung open her front door. She was still dressed in her leopard-print silk nightie, with matching dressing gown and eye mask. I didn't know what hairstyle she was treating us to today, because it was tucked away underneath a golden headscarf.

"Hold your horses, where's the fire? ...Oh, it's you two. What time of day do you call this?" she yawned.

"Erm, around eleven o'clock in the morning," said Dad.

"WHAATTT?!" exclaimed Auntie Sharon. "It can't be, it's too dark!"

"Maybe that's because you're still wearing your eye mask," said Dad.

"Oh!" Auntie Sharon ripped the leopard-print mask off. She looked like a bewildered cub.

"We can do this next week if you're not up to it today," said Dad.

The worms in my stomach knotted. I desperately wanted to spend time with Auntie Sharon. She was making me laugh already.

"Big night out. Leaving do after work," stumbled Auntie Sharon. "That'll teach me for bunking off my floristry lesson. Sunshine, learn from your Auntie Sha Sha and never be led astray." Auntie Sharon tapped at her nose.

I had no idea what she meant.

"Right, well, if you're sure?" said Dad, hesitating a little.

Once Dad had gone, Auntie Sharon swept me into her zebra-print living room, sticking the telly on.

"Make yourself comfortable while I zhuzh myself up a bit. My breath could knock out a herd of cows," she said, blowing into her hands and sniffing them with a pained expression. "I'll get Daz to come and sit with you if I can prise him out of his bedroom. He's probably still lost in the land of snore!"

I didn't really need the telly or Daz to entertain me. Auntie Sharon's living room is like entertainment in itself. If it's not the zebra-print wallpaper and rug, it's the coffee table, which has a giant silver hand for a base and a heavy-looking clear glass top on it. The hand reminded me of Grandad Bobby's hands: strong enough to hold anything up.

I wondered whether Daz spent so much time in his bedroom because of all the shiny and sparkling ornaments dotted all around their flat. One false turn could send them smashing to the floor, with only the hope of Auntie Sharon's plush white carpets softening the blow.

She appeared half an hour later, looking fully zhuzhed and wearing tight blue jeans and a white frilly blouse. A blonde bob, with a long fringe that fell to the side of her face, covered her left eye. She was also wearing the most gigantic pair of sunglasses I've ever seen.

"Sunny, your Auntie Sha Sha hasn't got the strength to take you shopping today, so we'll have to put up with the clothes you're in." Auntie Sharon sniffed in disappointment.

I wasn't quite sure what was wrong with the clothes I was wearing. I had on a blue sweatshirt with a white T-shirt underneath, blue jeggings, white trainers and a jacket. Mum insists on me dressing in layers as soon as she hears any weather presenter say "winter's on its way". If Mum had heard talk of changing my outfit, she'd have gone ballistic.

"How about the flicks?" said Auntie Sharon.

I gave her a side-eyed glance. "What are the flicks?" I was thinking Auntie Sharon was on about us doing some kind of gymnastics class, but I didn't see how that would be possible, not in those jeans at any rate.

Auntie Sharon released a high-pitched laugh and then held her head, as if the sound of her own voice was too much even for her. "Sorry, kid, it's the old-Hollywood in me. I mean the cinema, let's go watch a movie."

I'd never been to the cinema with Auntie Sharon before. I didn't mind, but I was kind of looking forward to our usual shopping trip, not for the clothes, but just to soak myself in the bustle of her. I was relying on Auntie Sharon to take my mind off my worries.

"Okay," I said, trying to sound enthusiastic. Auntie Sharon grabbed a pair of skyscraper black and white zigzag heels, and a black shaggy-haired jacket at the front door, ran into Daz's room to give him instructions for the day, and then we were off in a taxi to the cinema.

Auntie Sharon wore her sunglasses all the way through the movie. She grunted or burst out laughing at certain times — mainly when she woke up, briefly, from her nap. I ate my popcorn and had a drink while she snoozed.

"Ooh, I feel really refreshed. Wasn't Idris Elba brilliant?" she said as we emerged from the darkness of the cinema into the hazy afternoon sunlight. The actor Idris Elba wasn't in the film — not even doing a voice-over (it was an animated movie) — but I didn't say anything. I squinted, adjusting my eyes to the light. Auntie Sharon pushed her sunglasses up to the top of her nose. "What a gorgeous day, let's have a nice walk back to my place through the park."

"WHAT? IN THOSE HEELS?!" I shouted.

"Girl, shoes are my second skin. I could run a marathon in these. Come on, I'll show you." Auntie Sharon set off at a pace.

I was glad for the walk in the end. Seeing the changing colours of autumn and having the cool October breeze blow across my face felt very relaxing. Auntie Sharon chatted about her endless activities: her driving lessons, martial arts, and flower arranging. I didn't know how she managed to do all this, plus her proper job of managing people at the council.

"So, what's up, kiddo?" she asked. "Well, I say up, but if that face of yours plummets any further, we'll both end up down under in New Zealand."

"Can't you make Dad stay? I don't want him to work in Norfolk," I said. "Mum keeps telling him to go, but I don't think she really wants him to."

Auntie Sharon laughed wryly. "Hey, once your mum has made up her mind about something, that's usually it. She's got all the stubbornness of your Grandma Pepper, though she'd never admit it. Actually, the only person who could ever pull her up in her tracks is probably our mum."

My face crumpled.

"Look, I'm not going to lie, with everything that's happened to us over the past few months, it's a challenging situation. But you've got to take everything as an opportunity, kiddo. You see that dad of yours. He may act the goat, but he's a smart guy. And this chance opens up a whole new world for you all. Your grandfather always used to tell you to have your own adventures. Well, here's one about to start for your whole family!"

I was stunned at Auntie Sharon's wisdom. I hadn't thought about it like that before.

"Besides, it gives me a chance to unleash myself on Norfolk. You bet I'm going with you lot to check the place out. The locals won't know what's hit them!" Auntie Sharon smiled and so did I.

I wondered if I should tell her about trying to track down Grandma Pepper, but I wasn't sure. Auntie Sharon is a couple of years younger than Mum, so Mum has always looked out for her, despite their squabbles. I think sometimes Mum behaves like she's actually Auntie Sharon's mum too! Mum had to take on a lot of responsibility when Grandma Pepper went to live in Jamaica, when she and Auntie Sharon were teenagers. I think Auntie Sharon really misses Grandma Pepper, as she has a photo right next to her bed of the three of them: her, Grandma and Mum.

Auntie Sharon bent down and picked something up from the pavement, clutching it between two of her black and white lacquered fingertips.

"Find a penny, pick it up. All day long you'll have good luck," she said. "Or as your grandad would have said, 'Every mickle makes a muckle.'" Auntie Sharon rubbed the penny with a cleansing wipe from her bag, before handing it over to me with a grin.

"Thanks, I could do with a bit of luck," I told her.

Auntie Sharon whipped out another wipe from her

handbag and wiped down a bench before sitting on it. She gestured to me to sit next to her, kicking off her shoes, which sailed off into the nearby grass. "You want to get anything else off your chest?"

I spat it all out. I couldn't help myself. All my worries and fears spilled out like sweets from a jar. Moving up to secondary school; tests; Riley hating being in our charity stall group; Mum being sad; Dad working away; not having Grandad to talk to. Though I didn't tell her about the letter to Grandma Pepper in the end. I didn't want to pick at a wound that didn't need to be picked.

"What a long list of botherations," she sighed. "Listen, I can't fool you, lots of things have changed, and things are *still* changing. A terrible thing has happened to us in losing your grandad. It will take time for us to heal — and we'll all have to do it in our own way. Some of us will do it kicking and screaming, like me — and some will mourn quietly, like your mum. A lot is changing for you too. Not just changing schools. My little niecey-weesey is growing up — and that brings a whole heap of worries of its own. Life will always have its swings and roundabouts. But I want you to know, whatever happens, wherever you are in the world, I will always be there for you." Auntie Sharon let out a long, gooey sniff.

"Well, I'd rather the swings and roundabouts stay in the park where they belong, thank you very much," I said, pointing over to the play area.

Auntie Sharon smiled. "Look, Sunny, I want you to remember this piece of advice I'm going to give you right here and now, from this wise old saying: we run tings, tings nuh run we!"

"What does that mean?" I asked.

"It means we can't control everything, but where you do have some say, control your own destiny. First up, tell that Riley boy to get a grip on himself and stop being a fool. Work your hardest at whatever school you end up in, but don't stress yourself about tests, it's not worth it. Tests judge a moment in time, but they're not a judge of your character. And Evie falling off the bed was an accident, that's all. All you can do is do your best — hang onto the positives, wherever you can. You've got to look on the bright side."

In that very moment Auntie Sharon sounded just like Grandad Bobby.

"Look, over there!" she suddenly shrieked. I followed Auntie Sharon's finger over to a couple of black and white birds, playing together on the grass. "Two magpies mean joy," she smiled. "Come on, let's get back and we can order in some takeaway and eat it with Daz. That joy will do for starters."

Auntie Sharon rose from the bench and tippy-toed over to her shoes on the grass. As she stretched to put her shoes back on, she shrieked even louder.

"What's wrong?" I gasped, frightened that she'd done herself some damage due to the tightness of her trousers.

"I can't believe it," she said, swooping like a hawk and plucking something from the grass. "A four-leaf clover! A four-leaf clover!"

What was so exciting about a small piece of wilted grass?

"Three things in a row: the penny, the magpies, the clover. Our luck's going to change, you mark my words," exclaimed Auntie Sharon, with all the excitement of kids on a bouncy castle.

I hoped our luck would change.

28

AMERICAN CANDY

Spending time with Auntie Sharon gave me extra confidence that I'd done the right thing in trying to find Grandma Pepper. Maybe Grandma would be the luck we all needed.

If Grandma Pepper came back then Mum and Grandma could patch things up. Right now, it was impossible to do that with her so far away. Then Mum wouldn't feel as lonely without Dad. Grandma Pepper could probably make friends with Mrs Turner too, and they could keep each other company. The more I thought it over in my head, the more convinced I was that I'd done the right thing.

During half-term, every morning I'd rush downstairs

to see if I'd received a letter through the post, but there was nothing. I began to think that maybe the letters to Jamaica and America had got lost. I know I'd only sent the letters the week before, but Mr Chanda had assured me that the postal service moves fast.

But then, here's the thing — the rest of my family, they actually seemed a bit more relaxed as the days went by. Mum had started going out for evening power walks with my godmother Patsy, her best friend. Dad seemed to be more like his old, relaxed self too. He was chirpier, I couldn't deny that. It was as if my parents were both relieved that the secret was out about Dad working away from home.

I was getting on with **the Twinzies** again and I even showed them how to play the **A-to-Z All-Around-the-World** game. Mum still got them to keep up with their maths and reading during the break too, and I was their allocated helper. I didn't complain, I quite enjoy bossing them about — and we even used the new calculator!

Auntie Sharon and Daz came over to visit on Wednesday afternoon. Granny Cynthie and Grampie Clive were over, too. They'd brought **the Twinzies** home after taking them to **Wibbly Wobblies Play Centre**. We all lazed around the living room while **the Twinzies** invented a new game. Making the most of Daz's height, they got him to lift them up to the ceiling so they could see who touched it the fastest.

"I'll have a glass of the old vino pinko," said Auntie Sharon, stretching her body out with all the airs and graces of Cleopatra, across one of the living-room sofas. I kind of expected Daz to stop lifting **the Twinzies** and start feeding her grapes.

"You joining me, Chez?" said Auntie Sharon.

"Nope. Fit body, fit mind. Got to stay prepared." Had Mum actually turned into Miss Fairweather?

"Ah! Who needs wine anyway?" said Auntie Sharon. "I'm running on the juice of life. Something's changing, I can feel it tingling in my waters."

Dad coughed, nervously. Right on cue, the house phone erupted, making everyone jump. No one called the house phone any more, only Granny Cynthie and Grampie Clive and they were in the room.

Mum insists on keeping a landline in the house. "You never know when you'll need it," she says. Then she always goes on about how in the nineteenth century, two African-American inventors, Lewis Latimer and Granville T Woods, helped make important developments in the design of the telephone, to justify having one.

Sometimes I feel like saying, "I am very pleased for Mr Latimer and Mr Woods, but do you realize that we now live in the twenty-first century, and we don't need to use a phone that is attached to a wire?" But I never do.

Anyway, the phone was blaring. It took Dad around five of his long strides to make it out of the living room, step across to the hallway table, and answer the call.

All our heads swung in his direction.

"Who on earth is calling us on the house phone?" muttered Mum.

My point, exactly!

At first, Dad couldn't hear who was on the other end of the line. "It's a bit noisy, can you speak up, please?" Dad shouted, as if to give the person a lesson in how loudly they should actually be speaking.

But then Dad's face changed. It's hard to describe what happened to him. His expression became contorted and twisted. His voice sounded crackly and screechy — a bit like the bad phone line.

"Where? But how? No!... Yes!" Dad carried out most of the rest of the conversation in one-word answers. Whoever it was on the other end of the line had really hit their stride, and Dad was barely getting a word in edgeways.

Curiosity had now got the better of the rest of us and we'd all gathered in the hallway behind Dad, like a pandemonium of parrots on his shoulder, not even pretending to mind our own business. Something about the sound of the voice was familiar. Loud, but I couldn't catch the words. Dad was silent as he finally put the phone down. His hands were trembling.

"What is it?" Mum asked, urgency in her raised voice.

"It's...it's your mother," said Dad, quietly.

"What's happened to Mum?" screamed Auntie Sharon. "Is she sick? Oh no, is she—"

Dad stretched out his long arms and waved his hands in front of him to stop Auntie Sharon from saying any more.

"No, no! She is very much alive and in the present."

Everyone seemed confused. What had happened to Grandma Pepper? My heart started beating like a drum. **Thud. Thud. Thud.** Panic and hope filled each beat.

Dad looked straight at Auntie Sharon and Mum, who were hanging onto each other for dear life.

"For crying out loud, Tony, what a gwarn?" exclaimed Auntie Sharon.

"She's here. She's in England. Your mother's at Birmingham Airport!"

"Lord have mercy!" cried Granny Cynthie as Grampie Clive steadied her.

"What on earth is Pepper doing here?" We all swung round. It was Mrs Turner. Who let her in?

As we made our way back into the living room, with Mrs Turner following behind us like a bloodhound sniffing out a trail, the shock slowly set in.

"I've changed my mind," said Auntie Sharon, as Daz helped her back to the sofa. "Someone get that bottle open and pour me a glass of wine."

As for Mum, I'd never seen that expression on her face before. It was as if someone had tunnelled into her insides, removed every organ from her body and then inserted a metal pole so that she could still stand upright. She looked empty. Weak. Gone.

It was dawning on me that I was probably in the biggest trouble of my whole entire life.

All I could do was sit down, let myself be swallowed by Grandad Bobby's old chair and stare at the floor. This chaos was all my fault. I shouldn't have sent the letters.

"Do you think Grandma has brought some American candy for us? I hope she brings M&Ms," said Peter.

"Not now, Peter...and we can get M&Ms from Tesco's," Lena whispered through gritted teeth.

"Oh, yes," said Peter. "I forgot." Peter gulped as he scanned the living room and saw the shock set into everyone's faces.

If only I had listened to Charley and Arun, instead of thinking I was so right. Clearly, I was oh-so wrong.

29

GIANT BEE

When the taxi pulled up at our gate, less than an hour later, Grandma Pepper stepped out of it as if she was royalty. Not the Queen of England, but Queen of the World.

Her shoes were sharply pointed and as tall as skyscrapers. Amazingly, they were even taller and pointier than Auntie Sharon's heels! And her black hair, lit with streaks of silver, was swept upwards like a tall and swirling ice cream. She was wearing a glamorous tight-fitting knitted red dress, long, yellow trench coat, and a smart string of yellow beads around her neck, set off with bright red lipstick. She was so dazzling, that I wondered if Grandma Pepper realized that she was not on the set of a Hollywood film, but stepping onto a dreary, cloud-bitten street in England.

"Eh-eh, watch the poppy show!" whispered Granny Cynthie, meaning that she thought Grandma Pepper was being a bit of silly show-off. Granny was sneakily peeking at Grandma Pepper through the slats of the living-room blinds. "Is who mek dishcloth tablecloth?" she added. which I think was Granny's way of saying that Grandma Pepper thinks she's better than she is.

Mrs Turner wasn't as subtle. Somehow Dad had managed to wrestle her out of the house and back into her own home, but this had only spurred Mrs Turner on. First, a shadowy figure appeared at her front room window, then the net curtain lifted slowly, ending up completely over her head and, before you knew it, she was at the edge of her front garden with her shears, pretending to prune the now non-existent hedge.

Grandma Pepper seemed not to notice anyone as she floated towards our front porch like she was being carried in by an invisible force. Dad, Daz and the taxi driver stumbled behind her with all her suitcases and bags.

"Hello, everyone, I'm back!" she announced. Grandma spoke as if she'd only been away for a few days and not on the other side of the world like for **EVER**.

But I liked her immediately. She was extraordinary. Within minutes, Grandma was brightening a bleak time in our house — and that was just her clothes! Surely, she had the superpowers to make things better again?

"So, you too good to come meet me at the airport, Cheryl?" shouted Grandma Pepper at Mum. I don't think she was really shouting, just talking **REALLY, REALLY LOUDLY**. It's obviously a trait that runs in my family. "You always did have Tony wrapped around your little finger," she laughed. Well, I think she was laughing, but it was hard to tell, she sounded more like a mash-up between a whistling kettle and a dolphin.

Mum's back went up, a bit like a cat's does before it's going to have a fight. "You never told us you were coming until an hour ago! In fact, **NONE OF US** even knew where in the world you were."

This was awkward.

Mum started speaking in words that didn't contain any

vowels: "Phwwttt" and "brrrggg" and "grrrrr" spilled out of her mouth like bullets.

Auntie Sharon, maybe for the first time in her life, said nothing. It was as if she'd been electrocuted. Her blue wig was almost standing on end and her eyes looked like they were about to pop out of their sockets.

"Come to Momma," Grandma Pepper cooed to Auntie Sharon.

"Momma? Is that really you?" Auntie Sharon rose from her seat, stumbled over to Grandma Pepper and began sobbing into her shoulder.

"Come now, no tears, this dress cost me nearly three hundred dollars. Who has money to waste these days?" Was Grandma Pepper joking? I wasn't sure anyone could tell by the look of confusion on everyone's faces and the half-smile, half-grimace on Grandma Pepper's.

She peeled Auntie Sharon from her shoulder and turned on her giant heels to face her four grandchildren, like she'd not seen we were in the room all along.

"Darisuszkz?" Grandma Pepper marched over to him, reached up to his face and squeezed his cheeks.

"Ow!" said Daz. He started rubbing at his reddened face.

"Hush, you're a big man now, eh?" said Grandma Pepper.

She did the kettle-dolphin laugh again and then swung **the Twinzies** around one after the other, like rag dolls, pulling them into her chest and planting sopping great kisses all over their faces. Lena looked like she'd just been stung by a giant bee, lipstick marks printed all over her face. Peter looked as if he was about to throw up after receiving the kiss of life and being smothered by Grandma's boobies.

Grandma Pepper tried to do the same things to me. She couldn't quite manage to swing me like a discus, but the pulling into her chest and the slobbering kiss like a St Bernard was a definite repeat.

We cheered up after she plunged her long, colourful fingernails into her handbag and pulled out a huge packet of lemon sherbets. "A gift from the airport," she cried.

Then she bent down and did her best to do a hushed whisper. "I have lots more goodies for all of you in my suitcases." She winked as if this was a delicious secret between her, **the Twinzies**, Daz and me. It wasn't — the whole room heard. Mum gurned.

"You're all just such sweethearts!" My grandmother beamed. "And, Sunshine, how come you so tall already? How old are you now? Seven? Eight?"

"I'm t...ten," I stumbled. "Nearly eleven. In March. **The Twinzies**, I mean Peter and Lena, are six. They'll be seven in February." I didn't mean to tell Grandma Pepper our life stories, I was just so nervous.

Grandma laughed. "Good at your maths, I see."

"Phwwhtt! If you call the natural process of ageing being good at maths, then I guess so," blurted Mum.

The room's atmosphere plunged into shivery coldness.

This moment was difficult. Weird. Almost frightening. All of these things and then some. But there was also something about Grandma Pepper that was making me want more and more of her. I felt light and giddy, like I'd eaten too much sugar. She was almost delicious: smelling of talc and expensive perfume, and her lips tasted of cherries.

Grandma Pepper nodded politely at Granny Cynthie. "How y'all doing?" she said, in a long drawl that suddenly sounded very American. She turned to Grampie Clive and kissed him on his cheek, which made Granny Cynthie look as unhappy as Mum.

And then she spun around like a lighthouse's lamp looking for a missing ship.

"Where him is?" she asked, now sounding like a Jamaican. "Bobby come out and give your wife a kiss."

In that moment it felt like the earth had stopped turning. Everyone in the room jolted backwards, slowly moving against the force of gravity and time. As if I'd spun my globe really fast and jabbed it with my finger, causing it to come to a sudden standstill.

She didn't know.

My body was frozen but my brain was on fire, as I tried to take it all in. Grandma didn't know. She didn't know what had happened to Grandad Bobby.

30

THE LETTER

It took a hot minute for the grown-ups to adjust. The earth started spinning again, really quickly on its axis. Our brains tried to catch up so we could balance ourselves.

Dad suddenly swept all the children out of the room — even Daz — evacuating us from a sinking ship onto a lifeboat. "Women and children first," I imagined him shouting. Except the women — Mum, Auntie Sharon, Granny Cynthie — along with Grampie Clive and Dad, were left behind to break the news to Grandma Pepper about the tragedy that had happened to us.

Dad sent Daz, **the Twinzies** and me to wait in my bedroom until we were called back downstairs. Of course, we absolutely did **NOT** listen to this instruction.

Once we heard the living-room door shut, all four of us shot out of my room like cannonballs. We settled ourselves on the staircase, our faces pushed as far as possible through the banister, straining to hear anything going on inside the living room.

First, a mind-numbing silence...whispers...screams... loud cries...wailing. Long deep sobs seeped through the walls, out of the living-room door, and rose from underneath the floorboards. The air was thick with the sound of pain.

The Twinzies' lips started to quiver; they were going to lose it too. I nodded at Daz and he pulled Lena onto his lap. I patted Peter's back and then held his shoulders, pulling his body next to mine. I pointed to upstairs, because if **the Twinzies** wanted to go back to my room, we could. But they shook their heads furiously. So, we stayed. We listened. We waited.

After twenty minutes or so, Dad suddenly jerked open the living-room door, as if he was desperate to let fresh air flow in and wash over the anguish that was going on inside. We had been so absorbed in what was happening that we were caught **bang to rights**.

Dad looked at us and sighed but said nothing. He just waved his hand, indicating for us all to come down.

When we entered the room, Grampie Clive was passing something to Grandma Pepper in one of the posh glasses that usually live in our drinks' cabinet, where all the adult drinks are kept. She sipped it slowly and looked blankly out into the room.

Auntie Sharon was being comforted by Granny Cynthie. Daz went straight over to her and passed her a clump of tissues from the box on the coffee table. He sat next to her and put his long arm around her shoulder, like a comforting shawl.

And Mum? She was looking out of the front window, her back turned to us all. Body rigid. Head stiff.

Dad held **the Twinzies**, bringing them into his chest and rubbing their backs.

I just stood there. Gangly and awkward. Not knowing which way to turn. Where to place myself.

Grandma Pepper rocked back and forth gently in

Grandad Bobby's chair.

"But the letter," she whispered. "The letter didn't say anything about him being ill."

The world felt like it was caving in beneath me at this point. If only the floor would open up and swallow me whole. I had caused this. I was the worst person in the universe.

"What letter?" Mum swung round to face her mother. "If it's the will you're talking about, you don't have to worry, you've been well looked after," she said icily.

Grandma Pepper looked up and over at Mum, shaking her head. "No, no, no...I received a letter."

My heart started beating in my head.

"Please don't fight again," I cried out. "It's my fault, Mum. I sent Grandma the letter."

Everyone turned to look at me.

31

SAYING GOODBYE

"Sunny? What do you mean?" asked Dad.

I gulped, trying to produce a bit of water in my mouth to get my lips moving.

That's when I told them all about the letter, and sending it to Jamaica and America. About wanting to make things better. About wanting our new normal to be a nice new normal. About not wanting Dad to work away from home. How I'd begged Grandma to come back.

I thought I was doing the right thing. Charley and Arun had tried to warn me, but I wouldn't listen. I was so very, very wrong, when I thought I'd been so right.

"I'm sorry, Grandma Pepper, I didn't mean for you to

find out about Grandad in this way. I'm sorry, Mum. I'm sorry, Dad, and Auntie Sharon for sending the letter behind your backs."

No one said anything for a few moments and then Grandma Pepper spoke. "Child, what are you saying? I've received no letter from you. I've been on a world cruise for eight months and then got on a plane to come straight here. I haven't been back to the US or Jamaica."

Dad came over to me and crouched down to meet me face to face.

"Sunny, when did you send these letters?" he asked.

"About a week or so ago."

Dad smiled a little and drew me closer to him. "Sweetheart, even if the letters had reached your grandma, I'm sure even she would have called us first. None of this is your fault."

I clutched Dad, holding on tight around his neck, trying so desperately not to cry. But the more I tried, the more the tears tumbled.

"Do they not have phones on world cruises?" spat Mum.

Grandma explained that she had lost her mobile phone "somewhere between Nazareth and Bali" so she had no one's number. She didn't take her address book with her either because she'd had her phone. Grandma says she often disappears for a while to "de-stress" and that she didn't expect anyone to worry.

"I only managed to find your number because of a local telephone directory at Birmingham Airport. However, I did ask a good neighbour to send my post on to a friend for when I got to Europe," she told us. "And this is one of the letters I received…" Grandma Pepper reached into her designer handbag and took out the letter with a shaky hand.

"Cheryl, Sharon, your father wrote to me — and the letter only reached me a few days ago. As soon as I could get a flight, I came here to find him."

Grandma Pepper unfolded the letter and began reading.

"My sweetheart, Pep Pep,

I hope this letter finds you well and joyous. Keeping the free spirit about you that I have always so loved.

I have never said this as much as I should have

done, maybe us old folks don't do this enough, but I have always loved you — and will love you for all eternity. You have blessed me with happiness through our children, our grandchildren, and just by being you.

I will always care for you; you do not have to worry about anything.

Keep the fire burning in your belly and the passion flowing in your heart.

In health, and in sickness, I will always be yours.

I will stop writing now, before you tease me for being a silly, old fool!

Yours for evermore,

Bobby"

"He was saying goodbye," whispered Dad.

Tears fell onto the letter, but Grandma Pepper hurriedly dried her eyes. "I will not cry. I will NOT make this letter a soggy mess. It's the only thing I have left."

But it was too late. The living room flooded with all our tears.

32

GLAMOROUS "GLAMMY" PEPPER

It felt the right season for Halloween and bonfire night because it was very scary and explosive in our house. You could have cut the tension with one of Grandma Pepper's skyscraper heels.

Grandma was sleeping in Grandad's room, and Auntie Sharon and Daz had been round every day to spend time with her. Mum had mostly been trying to avoid Grandma. I just wished she would give her a chance, because a lot of things about her turned out to be fun.

By the end of half-term, these were some of the things **the Twinzies**, Daz and I had learned about our grandmother.

1. Her name is Glam-ma, Glammy, or Miss Pepper. We should never **EVER** call her Granny, Nan, Nanny, Nanna or anything else that makes her feel ancient.

2. Glammy only wears high heels — even to bed! Her slippers look like she could go to a nightclub in them without anyone batting an eyelid.

3. Glammy was in her seventies and a brilliant roller skater! She put on my

roller skates (as she has the same size feet as me) and rolled up and down our street. Forwards and backwards she went, spinning around in circles, and criss-crossing her legs. I don't think Mrs Turner could believe her eyes.

4. She is always singing. But not in an annoying way. Joyful sounds, like little birds chirruping, filled the house with life and prettiness.

5. She does brilliant impressions. My favourites are Dad scratching his head when he doesn't know what to say. Glammy says Dad's just like an old black-and-white movie star called Laurel somebody. She also does a great impression of my Grampie Clive, who shouts "What in the blazes?" on repeat.

6. She loves to shop *and* buy presents for us! Within two days of being here, she went out and bought Lena a magic set, Peter a tracksuit, Daz the latest trainers, and she got me a beautiful gold necklace with a little globe on it. She just gets us.

7. She always has handy "candy" in her handbag, which she carries around at **ALL** times, and she sneaks the little sweetie treats to us when Mum and Dad aren't watching.

8. She is **GREAT! AMAZING! FANTASTIC!** Just like Grandad Bobby.

However, the grown-ups were still struggling with ~~Grandma's~~ Glammy's sudden arrival and "her ways". When I wasn't supposed to be listening, I heard Mum tell Dad that Mrs Turner had spotted Glam-ma at the bedroom window in her nightie. Mrs Turner had said to Mum that "Someone of your mother's twilight years shouldn't be behaving and dressing like a twenty-something-year-old wannabe. She is no longer in the Tina Swift or Beyoncé age brackets."

I didn't know what that meant, but Glammy Pepper must have — and she must also have supersonic hearing — because she stormed into the room and accused Mum and Mrs Turner of "throwing shapes at her".

I wanted to tell Glammy that she should have said that they were throwing shade at her, not shapes, but I reckoned it wasn't the right time to interrupt. As cool as Glammy is, she still has that bit of oldness about her that gets being young a bit wrong sometimes. Just like Mrs Turner mistaking Taylor Swift for Tina Swift.

Every evening, after dinner, Glammy Pepper would go out into the garden and spend time gazing at Rose Pepper — the beautiful climbing rose that Grandad had named after her.

Even though it was nearly November, there was still one red rose, shining brightly, as if it had been purposely waiting for Glammy's arrival.

"I suppose everyone thinks me very selfish?" she said to me one evening, when she was outside looking at Rose Pepper. She tilted her head upwards and smelled the remaining rose. I didn't really know how to answer the question so I swerved it.

"How did you meet Grandad?" I asked her instead.

"Ha!" she said, disappearing into her memories with a smile. "I met him at a dance. He had such **joie de vivre**. Energy. Joy. I loved that about him and we were so happy. We enjoyed travelling, having fun. But then something changed. He wanted to settle himself, but when your mother and your aunt couldn't settle after we moved the family to Jamaica, he decided he wanted to root himself here, in England. When Dariuszkz, then you, and the twins came along — that was it. He was besotted with you all. He wouldn't leave you for a minute in fear of what he'd miss. I understand that now. Coming back and seeing you all so grown...I've missed out on so much."

"It's okay, Grandma, I mean, Glam-ma. Grandad always said that you needed to roam freely, like the wind."

Glammy Pepper smiled softly. "He probably knew me

better than I know myself."

I nodded. I felt that way about Grandad too.

"This time was different," whispered Glammy. "I was coming back. This time, I was back for good." Glammy wiped at her eyes. "Tell me more about what I've missed out on, Sunshine. What was your favourite thing to do with your grandfather?"

Lots of things tumbled into my mind at once. "Well… he used to take us to the park, and give us sweets, just like you do." I gave Glammy a little smile because I could see her eyes were wet and glistening.

"Go on," she encouraged.

"And he was so, so funny. He didn't do impressions like you do, but he told good jokes and stories, and he was so popular with everyone in our neighbourhood and at school. He used to teach us all rhymes and sometimes do little dances." I had to stop myself going on and on, but I found myself grinning. I hadn't talked about Grandad like this for ever. And it was nice to remind myself out loud of all the wonderful memories.

Glammy smiled warmly and dabbed at her eyes.

"Maybe I can help you make your cake for the charity day so we can do something together?"

"Oh," I hesitated. "Thank you ever so much, Glammy, but Granny Cynthie is going to make her Jamaican fruit cake with me, but I'm sure she'd love you to help too." I had to cross my fingers behind my back. My Granny Cynthie moves **ALONE**. The only reason she was letting me help her bake a cake was because I am her granddaughter and it was for the charity stall. Plus, she wanted to pass down her recipe to me, because Dad was always rubbish at baking.

Glammy Pepper looked a little disappointed, as if she really knew the truth of it all, but then she smiled. "Well, that would be nice. But I think there's only room for one Jamaican grandmother in a kitchen, and in this case that's Granny Cynthie. But she might have to cut back on the rum." Glammy winked.

Someone disturbed a plant pot on the patio and we both turned around to see Mum looking at us. She said nothing. Just frowned, folded her arms and stalked back into the house.

How could I get Mum to see that Glammy may have made mistakes, but that she was sorry? I knew she wanted to change given half a chance.

33

SPIRIT OF SPORTSMANSHIP

> **Person of the Day:** Footballer Shaka Hislop co—
> founded the charity Show Racism the Red Card
> in 1996. After he'd suffered racist abuse, he
> wanted to use the power of football to help tackle
> racism in society. Since its start, the charity's
> educational workshops have been attended by
> nearly one million individuals!

(Black History Month was over, but Miss Fairweather
said we would continue with the Black History facts on the
smart board until Christmas, as the topic was creating such
"positive vibes".)

With all the drama going on at home, I felt dizzy by the time I went back to school after half-term.

It was the start of November and also time for Dad to go to ~~Norfork~~ Norfolk.

Dad said he was going to tell work that he could no longer go, but Mum wouldn't have it. She told him: "You have to go" and "I will handle my mother".

On the way to school on Monday morning, I told Arun and Charley about Glammy's return. Evie was properly back on two feet now and walking with us as well. I couldn't text my friends during the holidays, for obvious **NO-PHONE REASONS**, and I didn't want us to be overheard on the landline, so they were eager to hear all about it.

"And what did she say?" asked Charley.

"And what happened then?" asked Arun.

"It sounds like a movie!" said Evie.

I guess it did. I told them about how guilty I'd felt sending the letters, but that Glammy Pepper hadn't even received them, and that she'd been away on a world cruise and had lost her phone so couldn't call. Boy, did I know what it was like not to have digits!

I had to forget about all the drama when we got into school. I just about had enough time to sneakily put a sticky note on Seraphina Adebayo's bag saying *"Your handwriting is lovely. So neat!"* as we were walking into class. After our warm-up morning exercises, Miss Fairweather wanted the class to talk about where we wanted the money raised from the charity day to go to.

A few people suggested giving the money to big charities that we had all heard of, but, after a bit of thought, everyone decided they wanted the money to stay somewhere in the local community.

Marcus said it would be nice to use the money to keep Beeches Park looking beautiful and Miss Fairweather said it was a lovely idea but that it was the local council's responsibility to keep the park clean and tidy.

Maya Watkins mentioned the local animal sanctuary, and everyone said "aww".

I suggested Mary Seacole House, the local hospice that Grandad Bobby had stayed in before he died, and everyone smiled and nodded at that.

Sheena Sandhu suggested a community bench in the middle of the town centre for tired shoppers to sit on, and that the school's name could be etched into it. We all said "ooh".

Izzy James said that she and her parents helped out at a local litter-picking group, Friends of Beeches Gardening, and that maybe the money could be used for new tools. We all nodded.

And then Evie put her hand up and said that the African Caribbean Centre that her dad volunteered at was raising money for repairs to their community hall, and that brought a few nods too.

I made a mental note to draw Izzy a sticky note with a bunch of flowers on it, Maya one with a cute puppy, and another for Sheila, with a bench — once I figured out how to draw one!

"Class, you have come up with some brilliant suggestions," said Miss Fairweather. "What we will do, in the spirit of sportsmanship, is make a chart for the wall and then you can all cast one vote each for your favourite choice over the next week."

On our way out to the playground at break, we were all excitedly chatting about the ideas and what we might vote for.

"How about you, Riley, what do you think?" I asked, trying, yet again, to get him involved.

"I dunno, not interested really. Your grandad was nice, so maybe the hospice, but not the African Caribbean Centre. My next-door neighbour says that charity begins at home. He said to make sure we give the money to something English."

We all shuddered to a halt then. Me, Charley, Arun, Evie. Even Carey, who is mixed race and Riley's best friend. Did Riley realize what he was saying? So much for Miss Fairweather talking about the smart board facts creating positive vibes.

When my Granny Cynthie uses the phrase "charity begins at home" she says it meaning that families have to look after each other to make sure their needs are taken care of first. But I think Riley's next-door neighbour meant that we should only look after some people, not everybody.

"That's racist, Riley," said Evie.

"No, it's not," shouted Riley.

"Yes, it is," said Arun.

"But the African Caribbean Centre is English," I said. "No matter what your neighbour says!"

"How can it be?" protested Riley.

"Right now, Riley, you're making me crosser than a hot cross bun!" shouted Charley.

"Ooh, I'm scared," said Riley, pretending to wobble his knees. But I could tell by the look on his face that he knew he'd said something wrong, even if he wasn't quite sure what. He started to push his football nervously from foot to foot.

"Didn't you hear Sunshine's speech at the Jubilee Assembly in Year Five?" continued Charley. "People from the Caribbean, like Grandad Bobby, came over to England to help this country. I think your neighbour said that because the people at the African Caribbean Centre are not white. But they've got a right to be here and have the charity money as much as anyone. You shouldn't treat people badly because they're different to you."

Riley shrugged and then looked down at the ground.

His eyes were glued to the football.

I was getting so mad that I could have burst. I'd finally lost my patience. But shouting at Riley wouldn't do any good. I had to "think on my feet". That's what Grandad used to say.

"Riley, who is your favourite footballer?" I demanded.

Riley shrugged. "Dunno!"

"It's Marcus Rashford," said Carey, getting into the spirit of things. Riley glared at Carey as if to tell him to shut up.

"What about your favourite team?"

"He supports Aston Villa," said Carey.

"And what about your favourite singers?"

"Riley likes Drake and Stormzy," said Carey.

"SO!" shouted Riley, scratching at his neck. "SO WHAT!"

"Don't you notice something about a lot of these people?"

Riley kept on with the shrugging.

I glared at him. "Charity begins at home, Riley! When you think about what that means, come find us."

We all stormed off then, and I turned and looked at Carey. "Are you coming with us?"

Carey bit down on his lip but shook his head and stayed with his friend.

"Do you think we should tell Miss Fairweather or Miss Peach about what Riley said?" asked Charley.

"Probably," said Arun.

"Definitely!" said Evie, who started to stomp away in the direction of the nearest teacher.

"No! Wait!" I called. "I don't know what's happened to Riley or why he's acting like this, but a telling-off might only make him worse." I probably wasn't saying the right thing, but I remembered Grandad Bobby telling me that racism is ignorance, and sometimes people have to be encouraged to change. Some people will listen and some people won't.

It just didn't make sense. Riley said he liked my grandad, but then said something horrible about people who he hadn't even met at the African Caribbean Centre. What was that all about?

"Let's give him one more chance and see if he comes

good with the baking. And if he's still acting the same way, then we'll say something to a grown-up," I said.

Everyone reluctantly agreed. We avoided Riley for the rest of the day and even Carey seemed quieter than usual. By the time I got home, I wondered whether I'd given the right advice. It's the first time I'd ever heard anyone say anything that I thought might be racist.

34

HUMMINGBIRD

Person of the Day: Vanley Burke is known as the "Godfather of Black British photography". He's taken photos of the everyday lives of Black Britons for more than 50 years. His mum gave him a "Brownie" camera when he was just ten years old – and the rest, as they say, is history – or maybe "clickstory"!

At home, things were still tense, so I didn't want to mention what Riley had said. Even though Dad FaceTimed us every day and asked about the charity day preparations, I hadn't said a word about the effect Riley was having on our team. Mum didn't need anything else on her plate; and Auntie Sharon was just so happy with Glammy Pepper being back that I didn't want to spoil it for her. I spent a lot of my time doodling little sticky notes to take my mind off my worry worms. I wondered if my excitement butterflies had finally been swallowed up by them.

At school I was an invisible contortionist, sticking my notes to people's bags, chairs and even their backs while they weren't looking. If I couldn't cheer myself up, I reckoned I'd try to cheer up other people.

I made a note for Carey of a boy with curly hair holding a trophy, the word **"champion"** and a football at his feet, which I stuck onto his coat.

My notes said different things like

"You're a star!" and **"Brilliant idea!"** with smiley faces and trophies drawn around the words for all my classmates and kids I knew in other years.

No one could figure out who the phantom sticky-note-artist was, not even Arun and Charley — and I played along with the mystery.

Then the funniest thing happened. Notes started appearing everywhere — not even written by me — and spreading across the school. People thanking each other and saying something nice about all sorts of things: a cool school bag; how well someone played football at lunchtime; even a note for the school cook to say how much someone loved her dinners, which came as a surprise to everyone — especially the cook!

One time, Miss Fairweather pulled her chair out from underneath her desk. She looked startled for a moment, took something from her seat, and then started reading from a little piece of pink paper. Her face gave nothing away, apart from one arched eyebrow. Then she hurriedly folded the note and shoved it into the pocket of her tracksuit bottoms and said no more about it.

Everyone was in such a good mood and seeing the joy on their faces boosted my spirits.

But then at home, a charity day baking **DISASTER** struck (almost)! Granny Cynthie's arthritis had flared up and Mum and Dad didn't think she'd be well enough to bake the cake for our stall. Dad asked her to tell us the measurements for the ingredients, but Granny Cynthie couldn't, she does everything by "using her judgement". Nothing is ever written down. She just does it!

"Don't worry, Sunshine, we'll think of a backup. We need to factor in a Plan B just in case Granny Cynthie isn't well enough when it comes to baking the cake in a couple of weeks' time, that's all," said Mum.

"Okay," I said weakly.

"I can be the 'Plan B'. I'll help Sunshine bake. It would be an honour," we heard a voice call.

Mum swung round to face Glammy Pepper. Mum looked at her as if a robber had broken into the house and was trying to take off with her jewellery. The butterflies flittered in my tummy. I really wanted Mum to let Glammy help.

"Oh, come now, Cheryl, why not? We'll come up with something so fabulous that the school will talk about it for years, won't we, Sunshine?" said Glammy Pepper.

I nodded enthusiastically.

"We can even do a practice run! Sunshine, this whole thing is about teamwork, right? So, bring your group of friends too, we'll make a day of it. Cheryl and Tony, you can go out for a nice lunch, and I'm sure Sharon will take the twins."

"No, no, it's fine." Mum winced.

"Come, now. I insist. It'll make a change to see you leave the house in something other than work clothes or cotton casuals. And a bit of make-up too, hopefully."

Perhaps it would have helped if Glammy had said something a little less insulting.

"Pleeeeasssssseeeeeee, Mum?"

Mum's eyes and head went a bit twitchy then, but she listened. "Okay, if you're sure."

"I'm sure," said Glammy Pepper.

I grinned from ear to ear. This was perfect!

For the rest of the weekend, I poured over Jamaicaninspired recipes with Glammy. We ruled out Easter bun, for obvious seasonal reasons. Banana fritters we decided were best served warm but we wouldn't be able to heat these up in an oven or microwave. Sweet potato pudding wasn't glamorous enough for Glammy's tastes, and coconut drops (which I love) had a high chance of getting stuck in people's teeth! In the end, we came up with something as exotic and as beautiful as my grandmother – a spiced banana and pineapple hummingbird cake. The recipe sounded delicious. It was perfect.

I was so excited at school on Monday morning. Mum had called Evie's, Arun's and Charley's parents and they all said it was okay to come over on Saturday at eleven o'clock to bake the hummingbird cake. Mum didn't have Riley's parents' number, so she was relying on me to get Riley to ask his parents himself.

We were good to go. But then Evie said something that made me worry.

"Are you sure about having Riley over? Suppose he says or does anything worse?"

I had to think — what if Riley did come out with something else in front of Glammy or my parents?

"I know," I said, wondering for a moment about what to do. "But can we give him one more chance? He might warm up a bit. Please, Evie!"

"Are you sure you don't *like* him, Sunshine Simpson!"

"No," I said firmly, especially not after what he'd said. I didn't really owe Riley anything. Yes, I'd known him for years, but we had never been best friends, and soon I probably wouldn't see him that much anyway, even if we ended up at the same secondary school. But I kind of didn't want to end Year Six on such a sour note. I guess, I wanted to help him.

"Okay, Saturday at eleven o'clock it is — with Riley." Evie sighed and rolled her eyes.

I marched over to Riley and gave him an offer he couldn't refuse. "Everyone's coming over to my house on Saturday morning to bake a cake. You're coming!"

Well, it wasn't the strongest offer, and he could have

refused it. After all, I didn't even know what Riley usually did on Saturdays. But he didn't say no. He just looked at me and said, flatly, "Okay."

And that was that.

35

CHOP! POUR! MIX!

On Saturday, my parents had made arrangements for **the Twinzies** to spend the day with Auntie Sharon, and then they were going for a nice lunch as Glammy had suggested.

The house was as shiny and as germ-free as an ice cube because Mum always insists on making sure every room is extra spotless if anyone outside the family comes over.

At eleven o'clock on the dot, Arun and Charley arrived, dropped off by their parents. Ten minutes later, Evie arrived with her dad.

I'm sure Mum left scratch marks when she finally let go of the front door. Dad almost had to lift her up like a mannequin and stuff her into the car.

"You go on now. That lipstick suits you," said Glammy. "Just a shade darker next time, I think. I'll look for an upgrade when I go into town next week."

Mum grimaced and left.

Glammy turned to face my friends and me. "I thought there were five of you?"

"Yes, we're just waiting for Riley," squeaked Charley, who looked Glammy up and down, her face filled with awe.

Glammy was dressed very glamorously, in a golden trouser suit, with sparkling rings on most of her fingers. I wondered if she had bells on her toes, too, like the old nursery rhyme. Glammy glanced at her matching gold watch and raised an eyebrow. "Riley's the rebellious type, huh, or just fashionably late?" she said to no one in particular. "Anyway, no matter, I approve of you four. You all exude a certain spirit I like."

Evie beamed at this. I could tell she'd already fallen for my grandmother in all her finery. You'll never catch Glammy Pepper in a "granny outfit" like comfortable slippers and a beige cardigan. No chance. Though one thing was for sure, Glammy was **NOT** dressed for baking.

"Should we start getting the basics out of the cupboard, while we wait for Riley?" I asked, slipping on an apron over my head.

Glammy's lips creased. "I'm not one for dealing with 'the basics', but I suppose we have to start somewhere."

We busied ourselves getting flour and sugar out of the cupboards, as well as a mixing bowl, spoons, and the weighing scale, while we waited. An **HOUR** later, Riley was dropped off by his mum. I answered the door, while Glammy "supervised" kitchen activities. Riley's mum waved happily from her car. "Bang on time," she called. Riley scowled at his mum.

"Riley, did you tell your mum we were meeting at twelve o'clock and not eleven o'clock? Were you deliberately trying to miss this?"

Riley shrugged. I couldn't be bothered to argue, so I let him follow me into the kitchen.

"Oh, it's the arrival of the king," said Glammy. She held her hand out towards him. Riley looked as if he didn't know what to do with himself.

"How'd ya do?" said Glammy, sounding a bit American and a bit royal at the same time. "My hand won't bite."

Riley took it, half shook it, and almost bowed — and then looked rather embarrassed, awkward and cross all at the same time.

"Tell me, Riley, are you hungry?" asked Glammy Pepper.

"Um, no, I don't think so, I've just had some crisps," replied Riley, hesitation in his voice.

"Come, a hungry man is an angry man, as the saying goes. Let's bake! It might cheer you up a bit." Glammy clapped her hands together and set us to work.

Arun, Charley, Evie and I stifled a laugh and Riley looked gobsmacked.

Glammy wasn't able to do any of the practical stuff, because she'd had her nails done the day before, but she happily ordered us about.

Charley and Arun were in charge of weighing out ingredients.

Riley was put in charge of cracking eggs.

Evie took on squeezing the lemon and chopping up

pineapples — with adult supervision from Glammy, of course.

I peeled and mashed the bananas.

We'd all be taking it in turns to do the mixing.

"Pick up your sticks and chop, pour, mix!" sang Glammy.

We did as we were told — but there was something off about Riley. He seemed stiff and awkward, like a rusty old door.

He hovered an egg over a bowl, as if he was going to drop it straight in instead of cracking it. Glammy saw him just in time. "Give it a little tap on the side of the bowl, then put your fingers gently into the crack and ease it open as carefully as you can," she said softly.

"Um, thanks. I've never really done this before... Martial arts are more my thing," said Riley, shyly and randomly.

"A karate-cook, I love that!" gleamed Glammy. Then she bent down towards Riley's ear and said, "Fake it till you bake it, sweetheart," and winked at him.

The rest of us pretended we hadn't overheard their

conversation and carried on. With clouds of flour billowing into the air, and the smells of banana, pineapple and Caribbean spices wafting between our noses, the kitchen looked and smelled like some kind of exotic food laboratory.

When it came to adding in the spices, Glammy wanted to do her own thing.

"Shouldn't we stick to the recipe?" asked Charley.

Glammy seemed to forget about her nails as she sprinkled "extra spice" into the mixing bowl. "Live a little...walk on the wild side." Glammy flashed her nails as if they were tiger claws and roared.

Riley burst out laughing!

Was Glammy weaving her magical charms on him? She'd certainly weaved them on the rest of my friends.

After we'd baked the cake and were waiting for it to cool, we made the icing with cream cheese, icing sugar and an orange. Glammy picked out the orange from the fruit bowl and held it out on the palm of one hand as if she was holding a crystal ball and then she explained to Riley how to zest it. I think we'd all realized by that point that this was Riley's first time baking, but it didn't matter, we were all having such a good time — especially as we licked the spoons and mixing bowl clean when we were done. And the finished cake smelled and tasted **AMAZING**. It was as if I was eating a slice of the Caribbean itself — sweet and spicy and fruity and just **YUM**!

We all sat around the kitchen table, slumped in a happy tiredness.

"Thank you, Miss Pepper," said Arun.

"Yes, thank you, we had so much fun," said Charley.

"It was the best!" said Evie.

We all looked at Riley, who swallowed the last of his cake with a satisfied gulp. "Yes, thanks," he mumbled. "That was okay."

Glammy Pepper's face sparkled. "Well, no one had more fun than me!"

At that moment, the kitchen door swung open, and Mum and Dad walked in. Dad's mouth flew into an "o" shape and Mum's eyebrows shot to the ceiling.

"What happened to my kitchen?" cried Mum.

We all looked around. Flour covered the floor, work surfaces, and even some of the ceiling. Our aprons and clothes looked like someone had dipped us all in white chalk.

"Come now, you have to let creativity express itself," said Glammy Pepper.

Mum glared. "Yes, all over my work surfaces, floor and ceiling, it seems."

Mum and Dad rolled up their sleeves and then we all set to work sweeping, scrubbing and tidying. Except for Glammy Pepper, who put the kettle on and made a cup of herbal tea.

Even Riley seemed happy to join in. He and Arun were practising the moonwalk as they slid backwards through the flour on the kitchen floor. Mum gave them one of her special looks — and they quickly went back to work with the broom and mop.

Riley was now like an obedient puppy and did everything as he was commanded.

"I thought you didn't like old Caribbean people," I whispered as we washed up.

"Well, your grandma doesn't look old or act old, does she? And I didn't say I didn't like... Anyway it was a stupid thing to say in the first place," he mumbled. He looked away from me and dipped his hands back into the suds.

It wasn't quite an apology, yet, but almost.

36

SORRY

Person of the Day: Dame Commander Pat McGrath DBE is considered to be one of the most influential make-up artists in the world! She's worked with really famous people in fashion, like a designer called Giorgio Armani, and with top fashion magazine *Vogue*. She's known as a "true creator and innovator".

At school on Monday morning, there was a yellow sticky note on my desk. It simply said "Sorry" and had a colourful bird with a long bill drawn on it — a hummingbird! I looked over at Arun, Evie and Charley — and they flapped notes in the air, too. No one had to guess very hard who the notes were from. I glanced over at Carey, and he held a yellow sticky note in his hand as well. Riley kept his head down.

After we took the register and did our stretches, it was time to announce who we were going to give the charity day money to.

Miss Fairweather coughed dramatically. "We have a split-decision! Otherwise known as a tie. If I may dip further into the ring of boxing references: in the blue corner, we have the animal sanctuary, and in the red corner, Mary Seacole House hospice! ...The crowd went wild!"

The class was completely silent. Not because we weren't happy for the chosen charities, but because we didn't know what Miss Fairweather was talking about. She sighed. "That means the money will be split between the animal sanctuary and Mary Seacole House hospice — and you can clap now."

We all immediately clapped and cheered — though Evie did look a little disappointed that she hadn't "won" this one. I was delighted that part of the money raised would go to the hospice though.

And then the most unbelievable thing happened.

Riley put his hand up. "Do you think we could invite the people from the African Caribbean Centre to come to the charity day?" he asked, sounding a little sheepish.

Miss Fairweather beamed. "What a fabulous idea, Riley. Well done! More people to add to the festive cheer."

Riley tried hard to swallow his smile. "It's just an idea," he said, shrugging his shoulders, like he didn't care that he'd come up with it.

"I can get my dad to ask the patrons," said Evie, with a broad beam stretched across her face. "I bet they'll love it!"

When we went out to the playground at break, Arun, Charley, Evie and me all went up to Riley.

"That was a really good idea, Riley," I said.

Riley put his head down and started to walk away. He then turned back round to face us. "I'm sorry," he said.

"Hmph! I should think so," said Evie, folding her arms. Charley looped her arm into Evie's.

"Like I said, I'm sorry," said Riley. "I'm sorry for what I said about the African Caribbean Centre. And I'm sorry for being so annoying about baking cakes and for not wanting to be in the group in the first place... I just missed Carey and I hadn't baked cakes before... Okay?" Riley had turned as red as fox fur after this confession.

Evie didn't say anything else. She just nodded and said gently, "Okay."

Riley gave a slight smile before turning to me. "And, Sunny, you may as well bring Miss Pepper to the charity day as well."

He walked away. Evie, Charley and Arun smiled — and so did I.

I spent a lot of time with Glammy Pepper as the rest of November flew by. We painted each other's nails, and

Glammy gave me a make-up tutorial. She didn't seem to mind, much, that she looked a bit like a clown when I'd finished with her face. I thought that blue eyeshadow, rosy-red cheeks and bright-red lipstick spread thickly across her lips almost looked quite nice. We fixed each other's hair, too, and I told her about how I "accidentally" cut my hair off in Year Five.

"Daring!" smiled Glammy, as she used a tail comb and gel to fix my edges perfectly into place.

Spending time with Glammy took my mind off Dad being away and reminded me of being with Grandad Bobby. Mum busied herself around the house and made excuses every time I asked her to join Glammy and me. Her face just grew more and more puffed up like a pufferfish.

On one of the days, I even told Glammy about what Riley had said about the money raised from the charity day only going to English charities.

Glammy sighed. "Did you give that boy a piece of your mind?"

I shook my head, guiltily. "I tried to find another way."

Glammy stopped fixing her make-up and turned away from the mirror to face me. "You know, your grandad used to say, 'don't trouble trouble, until trouble troubles you, for you will only double trouble and trouble others, too'."

"What does that mean?" I asked, playing the rhyme over in my head.

"It means your grandfather always tried to find the gentle way out of a problem, because he realized that we're all capable of making mistakes and wrong turns — whereas I tend to go straight for the fight. 'If we were all perfect to begin with, then how would we grow?' — that's what he used to say. You tried to take the peaceful route, just like your grandfather would. However, in this case, you should probably have told a grown-up sooner."

"But it's turned out okay. Riley apologized, and even asked for the patrons at the African Caribbean Centre to come to the charity day as well," I said. I didn't want Riley to get into any trouble, and as far as I was concerned the case was closed. "And you helped a lot to change his mind, Glammy. Riley really likes you!"

This seemed to please Glammy. She smiled radiantly.

"The older the moon, the brighter it shines," she said. "Still, right is right and wrong is wrong. Trust me, I know some things about being right, but mostly about being wrong. As you say, it seems to be resolved now, but if anything like that ever happens again, or worse, you speak up quick, you hear?" Glammy turned back to the mirror, looking a little sad. She put some more make-up on.

I nodded. "Yes, Glammy, I will."

Maybe I had done the wrong thing by not telling on Riley, I wasn't sure. But one thing I did know was right — Glammy's personality was bigger and brighter than any moon I'd ever seen.

37

OUT IN THE COLD

As December arrived, we all sat down for Sunday lunch with Auntie Sharon and Daz. There wasn't room for all of us at the dining-room table. It was Mum, Dad, Glammy Pepper, Auntie Sharon, Daz and me around it — so I felt especially grown-up. **The Twinzies** sat next to us at a fold-out table with plastic cutlery and paper plates. They pretended they were at a picnic, because that's **the Twinzies** for you.

Dad asked about the charity day and I told him, excitedly, about The Pudding Crew's plans — but then I remembered he wouldn't be there, he'd be doing maths in Norfolk. My face dropped.

"I wouldn't miss it for the world," said Dad. "How about I book the day off? I'm sure that will be okay."

I almost clapped with joy.

"Will there be any entertainment?" asked Glammy.

I hadn't thought about that. Besides, weren't all the different stalls entertainment enough?

"Come now, it's Christmas. Maybe a few carols playing in the background. Give the thing some flavour, hey?" Glammy suggested.

"Or maybe you could sing, Glam-ma?" said Lena.

"Ooh, yes, 'Jingle Bells'? I like that one!" added Peter.

That was pretty good thinking from **the Twinzies**.

"You could sing and take requests and raise more money for the charities, Glammy! You'll be great!" I cooed.

"Why I'd be delighted," said Glammy, in her Jamerican drawl. She put her hand to her heart and gave out the warmest of smiles, showing off her incredibly polished, white teeth.

"Ooh, and Mrs Turner is a good singer. She sang for us in the summer, and she was great. Maybe she could help out, too? I think she'd like that," I said.

"Really?" said Glammy, her lips suddenly ruler-straight. "Maybe, but I kind of like to go my own way. Do my own thing."

Mum uttered something. Almost like a grumble or a low rumbling cry of pain. Maybe Mum was saying "brrrr!" because the room suddenly felt very cold.

"Hmm…you don't need a knife to cut this atmosphere do you, Cheryl? You could do that with one of your looks alone," said Glammy. "Why bring the mood down with your sulking?"

That was just about enough for Mum. She couldn't hold it in any longer. She exploded like a cork blasting out of a fizzed-up bottle of pop.

"I'll tell you about bringing the mood down. We've all been left to manage while you…YOU sailed off around the world like Phileas Fogg! 'Going your own way' and 'doing your own thing'. But now here you are, the Queen of the charity day. It's unbelievable! Everyone thinks you're so dazzling, with your charm and your gifts and your trinkets, but you don't dazzle me."

"Chez, don't," hissed Auntie Sharon.

"I'm sorry, Sharon." Mum looked down at her shaking hands and whispered something that I could just about pick up. "I wish...I wish..."

Grandma Pepper sipped calmly from her glass of cucumber water. "The cock's mouth killed cock, Cheryl. You really need to be careful about what you say in front of the children, otherwise it will haunt you."

Mum stared at Glammy Pepper, shaking her head. "You really are something else."

With Glammy back, I'd hoped that the hole in the roof of our family would be fixed, but the roof was now collapsing around me. This whole thing was working more for me than it was for Mum and the sinking feeling made my chest ache.

Instead of herding us upstairs, Dad told us kids to put our coats and gloves on and then sent us out into the garden like pets needing a wee.

"Play catch or something with the kids for ten minutes will you, neph?" Dad said to Daz.

It was **DECEMBER**! The only thing we'd be catching outside was pneumonia. We were all, literally, out in the cold. Mind you, it was probably warmer outdoors than it was in the dining room.

There was no need for Dad to clear us out. We aren't fools. It wasn't hard to guess what Mum hadn't finished saying...

She'd wished Glammy Pepper had never come back in the first place.

My heart plummeted, along with the temperature.

While Mum was in her bedroom, Glammy Pepper packed a couple of suitcases and disappeared into a taxi with Auntie Sharon and Daz. My eyes filled with tears. Glammy was leaving us all over again.

"Hush now," said Glammy, kissing me and **the Twinzies** on our heads. "I'll see you at the charity day. I promise you I'll be there for that. And I'll call."

"But I don't have my own phone." I whimpered.

Glammy smiled and caressed my face.

Mum seemed much calmer by the time she came downstairs, after Glammy had gone, which made me feel a little bit cross. Why couldn't Mum see the good in Glammy? Why was she always so keen to search for the bad in her? Glammy had filled our home with life and light again. Now the space felt empty without her. Why was Mum so stubborn? Why couldn't she see that we needed Glammy? *I* needed her.

Dad and Mum sat down to talk to **the Twinzies** and me around the kitchen table.

"Your grandmother will be staying with Auntie Sharon and Daz for a while," said Mum.

"Why?" asked Peter. Had he not seen and heard the fireworks in the dining room earlier on? Lena and I gave him a look.

"Well, your grandmother and I haven't been getting along too well, and we need some space to work things out," said Mum.

"How can you work things out if she's not here?" asked Lena.

Mum was stumped by Lena's question.

"Because sometimes a change is as good as a rest, if I may reach for a fitting cliché," smiled Dad. He looked tired, as if he'd been wrestling with two alligators and lived to tell the tale.

"Is that why you're working so far away from home, because a change is as good as a rest?" asked Peter.

Now Dad was stumped for an answer and began rubbing at his head.

"We're just trying to build a better future for all of us," said Mum, sounding like a robot again. She smiled at Dad, but it was kind of a weak smile.

Mum then looked at me. "Sunshine, you're very quiet. Do you want to say anything or talk about this?"

After a few moments I said, "Why can't we just live?" I didn't know what I was saying really, but all I felt was responsibility. Like somehow this was my fault for wishing so hard for my grandmother to come back. "For so long I've wanted the world to stand still. For change not to come. But it does come. I can't stop it. I realize that now. Why can't you just get along — before it's too late? That's what Grandad would have wanted — I know it! He enjoyed life — and we should too. Glammy helps us. Why can't you see that, Mum?"

Mum gulped. I thought she was going to tell me off, but she didn't. "Ah, Sunny, you're growing up so, so fast. Do you remember how I said to you a while ago that life isn't always as simple as black and white?" I nodded. I did remember. "Well," continued Mum, "a lot of water has passed under the bridge between your grandmother and me. It's all a bit...pear-shaped. And I realize I'm speaking in a whole heap of clichés right now too, but I don't know what else to say — except for what a wise young lady you've become."

Everyone was always telling me how wise and grown-up I was, but then why would no one ever listen to me if that was really true? I wanted to beg Mum to at least try with Glammy Pepper, but I didn't want to upset her any more.

"Look, I am so sorry about what happened earlier," said Mum. "You're right, Sunny. Let's try our best to get into the Christmas spirit and have a good time — like your grandad would have wanted." Mum smiled.

For a moment, I thought Mum was going to say that she was going to get on the phone to Glammy Pepper and ask her to come back to our house, but she didn't. I smiled back at Mum, but inside I felt like crying.

CHARITY DAY!

People of the Day: Even though people who came to Britain from the Caribbean between 1948 and 1971 are known as the Windrush generation, the Windrush was not the first ship to bring people over after the war. In fact, people of colour, from countries across the world, have been making a contribution to Britain for many centuries. You can even find the statue of the influential African-born Roman Emperor Lucius Septimius Severus, who lived and died in England, in the British Museum, London.

Two weeks later, and just a week before Christmas, the charity day finally arrived.

I'd spoken to Glammy on the landline (okay it does have its uses) every day in the lead-up, and **the Twinzies** and I went over to visit her at Auntie Sharon's. But I desperately wanted her home with us. It was as if every time I spoke to her or saw her, I wondered whether it would be for the last time. I was scared to lose her all over again. But as we remade the hummingbird cake together for real this time in Auntie Sharon's kitchen, as Granny Cynthie was still not up to it, I decided just to enjoy every moment with her. At least she'd promised me that she'd come and sing a few carols at the charity day. I couldn't wait for everyone to hear my Glammy sing. I knew she'd set the place on fire with her voice.

My class spent the morning preparing our stalls in the school hall. We used the big tables that we usually used in the canteen. But we made them look special. Each group took charge of how their stalls were dressed. The only thing each one had in common was the lovely red tablecloths that Miss Peach had brought to give the tables an extra bit of Christmas sparkle.

Both **The Lemon Heads'** home-made lemonade and

hot chocolate stall, and The Puzzlers' bric-a-brac stall had colourful bunting draped from end to end. The Painted Faces' stall wore a Christmas garland of pine cones and holly, and The Slam Dunkers wrapped their basketball hoop in red and white tinsel. The Cocobolas' coconut shy and tombola stall was draped in bunting intertwined with tinsel. And our Pudding Crew stall had an extra magical touch, with little white fairy lights, hanging from end to end, twinkling like stars.

The Pudding Crew bakes looked so tempting sat next to each other on the tablecloth. I could have dived in and eaten the lot! Arun had his carroty gajar ka halwa, Charley had made Irish apple cake and oat cookies, Evie baked Trinidad (Trini) sponge cake and coconut fudge — and I had brought mine and Glammy's hummingbird cake.

Riley had come good too. He'd made the most delicious-looking Victoria sponge with his mum. Jam and

cream oozed out of the sides and there was a dusting of icing sugar on top that looked perfectly Christmassy. Riley had gone from no baking at all to a master baker in a few short weeks!

Something else had happened to Riley over that time too. At first, I'd thought Glammy Pepper had told Mum and Dad about what Riley had said about the money raised from the charity day only going to "English charities", but it turns out it wasn't Glammy Pepper who mentioned anything — it was Carey, Riley's best friend.

Carey had told his mum and Carey's mum had spoken to Riley's mum. Riley's mum and dad then called all our parents and apologized. They said they were used to their neighbour saying "funny things like that" when they spoke to him over the garden fence, but they'd always just ignored him. They "hadn't dreamed that Riley would repeat anything" — and now they promised to say something, "call it out", if ever they heard their neighbour say anything like that again. My parents said they appreciated the phone call.

After we'd done all the setting up of our stalls, Miss Fairweather called the class to the back of the hall. I was worried she'd make us drop to the floor and do some exercises to "limber us up" for the afternoon ahead, but she didn't.

"This!" she said, stretching out her arms. "YOU. DID. THIS." For a moment or two, we wondered whether we were in trouble, but then Miss Fairweather started clapping, so we all started clapping, because she was clapping. In her own way, I think Miss Fairweather was saying she was proud of us, so overwhelmingly proud, it seems, that she forgot to say anything sporty or make us do any exercise — which was another bonus.

After the clapping, we all fell silent and marvelled at our stalls. They looked "very professional" as my parents might say. Magical with the fairy lights, tinsel, garland and bunting.

After lunch, the hall was filled to the roof with chatter as Years Four and Five came to take part in the fun. We sold cake slices and Arun's little pots of gajar ka halwa for one pound each and the oat cookies and fudge pieces for fifty pence each. As we took the money and gave out change, we felt like our very own bosses.

The face-painting went down a treat, too. Butterflies and tigers mingled with lions and unicorns, who drank lemonade and hot chocolate, ate puddings, bought books and jigsaw puzzles, and had a go at shooting hoops or smashing coconuts.

The grown-ups came later in the afternoon. Mum and Dad brought Mrs Turner with them. Grampie Clive pushed Granny Cynthie in a wheelchair. Granny's arthritis was still pretty bad, but amazingly she had managed to "rustle up a little something". She'd baked a small cake and contributed it to a Christmas hamper that was going to be raffled at the end of the afternoon.

Auntie Sharon arrived in a glittery black jumpsuit, but there was no sign of Glammy Pepper. I craned my neck around the hall. Maybe I hadn't spotted her, but Glammy is so bright, both in her clothes and personality, that in my heart I knew she wasn't in the room. Had Glammy just left, like she always did? Maybe Mum had been right all along.

I cheered up a bit when I spotted Evie's dad. He'd arranged a minibus to bring along some of the patrons from the African Caribbean Centre. They were dressed so elegantly, turning out in their best dress for the occasion. The men wore suits with their favourite ties and pork-pie hats, and the ladies wore their shiniest sparkly outfits and Sunday church hats. They were so pleased to be invited and bought lots of cake from our stall — and Riley even suggested we give them a discount.

The queue was so long for the cake stall that I didn't even have time to talk to my family. I wanted to ask Auntie Sharon what had happened to Glammy Pepper. If she didn't turn up, this would be another reason for Mum refusing to patch things up. I felt myself getting more and more wound up.

After a while, there was a lot of shuffling and activity at the front of the hall. People in colourful tropical shirts walked onto the school stage carrying big steel drums, which are also called **pans**. The lights lowered and then a familiar person in a black jumpsuit, matching Auntie Sharon's, walked onto the stage, shimmering in the spotlight. It was Glammy Pepper!

"My name is *Miss* Pepper Starr, otherwise known as Sunshine's glam-mother, and I'm so glad to be here. Let's make this beautiful occasion extra festive," she said, speaking soothingly into a microphone. The steel band started to play and Glammy began singing "All I Want for Christmas is You" by Mariah Carey. Now I could see why my grandmother's singing has taken her all over the world. Her voice filled the room with the most wonderful sound like she was an entire choir singing all by herself — I was sure the roof was going to lift off and sail away with the beat. And who knew that her "stage name" was Pepper Starr!

"This next song is dedicated to someone very, very special," she said. "I hope you all remember Sunshine's grandfather Bobby," she said. "He was such a special man and I hear there's a special singer here today, too. Maybe she'd like to give me some help?" Glammy Pepper stretched her hand out towards the audience.

All I could see was Dad helping a lady up, with neatly set brown curls and a tweed suit – it was Mrs Turner!

They both started singing Grandad Bobby's favourite Christmas song, "Mary's Boy Child". Glammy Pepper held Mrs Turner's hand as they sang and looked towards Mum, who clasped her hands to her chin and nodded at Glammy Pepper. She smiled and nodded back at Mum.

Some people in the hall started to swing and sway, while others continued to browse our stalls while enjoying the music. The tinkly, jangly notes of the steelpans made it feel like we were in the middle of a Caribbean Christmas.

It turns out that Dad had secretly arranged with the school for Glammy to surprise everyone and Evie's dad had not only arranged the minibus for the patrons of the African Caribbean Centre, but for the steel band to play too.

One of the Caribbean patrons suddenly got cramp as they swung their arm too vigorously at the coconut shy. Miss Fairweather rushed to

306

their aid, helping them to do some stretches to ease the cramping — and then some of the others joined in with the stretches in time to the music. Miss Fairweather was so good! So kind and gentle.

When she came over to the cake stall to check how we were getting on, I thought I might ask her something. "Miss Fairweather, Evie's dad says that the African Caribbean Centre can always use helpers. Why don't you do an exercise class there?"

Miss Fairweather's cheeks tinged pink. "Well…I'm not so sure about that," she blustered.

"But you're a great athlete. I bet you could have been an Olympic champion!" I said.

Miss Fairweather's jaw nearly hit the floor and I wondered what I'd done wrong. And then I realized. I threw my hand up to my mouth.

"It was you, wasn't it? You wrote the note and left it on my chair. I couldn't work out if someone was making fun of me…or…or was just genuinely being kind." Miss Fairweather's voice tailed off.

"But you *are* a great athlete, Miss Fairweather. I mean

sometimes you can be a little…intense…but I think that's because you were born to be a champion." I expected her to kick-off then and give me a million and one star jumps to do. But before she had time to respond, Evie's dad came up to us.

"Miss Fairweather, you're certainly putting everyone through their paces," he said, smiling.

"I was just saying to Miss Fairweather how great it would be if she did an exercise class at the African Caribbean Centre, Mr Evans. I mean Carl," I said.

Carl grinned. "Fantastic! Just what we're looking for! When can you start?"

"Well…yes…okay…I'd love to!" said Miss Fairweather. "But not until after the holidays as I'll be on a bobsleighing course in Germany over Christmas."

Only Miss Fairweather!

Everyone cheered at the end of the mini concert. Then Miss Peach got up onto the stage to make a speech. After all, she is the assistant head teacher of Beeches School now.

"Children, friends and family members. Well, what can

I say, except thank you to Year Six for organizing this wonderful occasion. Each one of you will have a glowing report sent to your new secondary schools."

"Hear, hear!" shouted someone in the hall wearing a pork-pie hat.

"And may I say an extra special thank you to our new friends from the African Caribbean Centre and steel band for joining us — and to Sunshine's grandmother for leading the school in such rousing Christmas songs."

Everyone gave a hearty round of applause.

"One last thing before we wrap up for Christmas, if you'll pardon the pun," said Miss Peach, who seemed very tickled by her ~~bun~~ pun. "I'd also like to mention the lovely sticky-note messages that have decorated our building over the past few weeks and filled the school with such joy. Mrs Honeyghan and I have been talking about how we can translate this uplifting idea into something more sustainable, so that we can carry it forward for years to come. We've decided to have a dedicated space on the celebration wall in the school hall for a digital board where our office staff have very kindly offered to type up your notes of thanks.

Whoever the secret person is who came up with this idea, you have contributed to a delightful legacy and you should feel very proud."

Everyone cheered, including me. I couldn't believe what Miss Peach had just said. I felt completely amazed that those little sticky notes had turned into something this big.

I looked around the hall. Everyone was enjoying themselves. Miss Fairweather was beating everyone, including Dad and Mr Evans, at the basketball stall. One of the steelpan musicians was teaching Auntie Sharon how to play a few notes, and Mrs Turner, Mum, Evie's mum and Glammy Pepper all stood together sipping hot chocolate. I almost gasped at the sight. Grandad Bobby would have loved this moment.

"What you thinking about?" asked Riley, who was suddenly standing right next to me.

"I don't know...just how I wish when you find a happy moment that you could freeze it, so it always stays the same."

"Do you wish you could stay young for ever like Peter Pan?" he asked.

I nodded.

"Me too," he said, quietly. "I wish we could stay at Beeches Primary for ever."

I couldn't believe it. Big, tough Riley was scared to move on and start high school too!

"But you know what?" I said, smiling and hitting Riley playfully on the shoulder. "My grandad would've told me that life's an adventure and that you just have to carry on and live it."

"Your grandad was nice," said Riley.

"Thanks," I said. "He was the best."

Once the charity day was over and we were getting ready to go home, Dad called the family over into a huddle. He had his arm around Mum's shoulder.

Dad cleared his throat. "I thought I'd share some news that I couldn't wait to tell you... As you know, I've been offered this great opportunity over in Norfolk."

Was Dad about to tell us we were moving there? My heart skipped about five beats.

"But something didn't feel right — and today has confirmed that feeling," he continued. "Home is where the heart is and that is right here with you all... I've pulled out of the placement in Norfolk, one of the other accountants will take over. I'm going nowhere."

"But what about the Norfork spider turkeys?" asked Peter.

"Well, how about we go on holiday there to try and find some? It's still a stunning place." Dad grinned.

"But, Dad," I started, desperately hoping that I wasn't dreaming. "This is a great chance for you. Won't your boss be really cross?"

"I'm more concerned about what I'm missing out on when I'm not with you," said Dad. "It'll be okay — life finds a way of working itself out in the end. And, if I really have to, I'll find a new job right here that's even better."

"Too right," cried Auntie Sharon. "The wind's changing, I can feel it."

My family started to laugh and cheer, whoop and holler. And if felt like the steelpans had jumped inside of me and started playing a tune that made my butterflies have a massive **PARTY**!

Now Dad would be staying home, all there was to do was keep working on Mum and Glammy Pepper.

39

BORN IN A BARN

"Well, the charity day was a real success," Mum declared when we were home.

"That Miss Fairweather's a tough one though," said Grampie Clive, cracking his neck. "She was teaching some of us old-timers exercises before she starts her class at the African Caribbean Centre in the new year."

"Only one cure for achy limbs," Dad said, as his mobile phone started to ring. "One medicinal hot pot of tea coming up, after I take this call."

Grampie Clive, Granny Cynthie and Mrs Turner settled down to watch a Christmas movie on the telly. **The Twinzies** went off to find Dad to make sure he didn't get distracted by his phone call and forget his tea-making duties and Auntie Sharon went home with Daz to get ready for her "hot date". It turns out that Dennis, her driving instructor, wasn't just nervous due to Auntie Sharon's driving — he also had a massive crush on her! He'd waited until after her driving test to tell her. She passed, by the way! (Yes, definitely a Christmas miracle.)

Glammy Pepper had left the charity day slightly earlier than us and headed back to Auntie Sharon's place in a taxi. She said she was tired after all the singing.

"Are you happier now?" Mum asked me.

I nodded. "Yes, I think so."

"You think you are?"

"Is it wrong to feel happy again?" I asked. "I mean, now we don't have Grandad."

Mum smiled gently. "When someone really special dies, sometimes you can feel guilty about finding joy in new things. There are times you'll feel sad, but then there are other times you'll smile and laugh at memories, both old and new — and that's more than okay. Besides, I know that your grandad would have been so proud of you, especially after a little bird told me a secret about who it really was who'd started off the sticky-note craze at school."

Miss Peach had promised that she wouldn't tell, but as it was something that made Mum smile from ear to ear, I decided to be glad about it.

"I really want you to be happy again, Mum. I wanted to bring Glammy Pepper home, because even though I know things aren't the same without Grandad, I thought it might help to bring everyone together again."

Mum shook her head. "You are *not* responsible for making me happy, Sunshine. I can see you were trying to make it all better, but these wounds will take a bit of time to heal. Probably lots of time."

I nodded, trying to understand.

"Look," said Mum, suddenly brightening. "I know you desperately want things to work out with your grandmother, and I can tell she's having quite an impact on you."

"Not in a bad way, though," I said, jumping to Glammy's defence.

"No, not in a bad way. But the thing I've noticed most

is the impact you're having on *her*."

"What do you mean, Mum?"

"How she brought Mrs Turner up onto the stage today to sing with her — well, that was quite a surprise," continued Mum. She bit her lip. "Look, you've gone to so much trouble and tried so hard to make everyone happy, I've decided to give it a go. I've been thinking that I should spend some time with your grandmother and try to find a way forward."

"All you can do is try." I beamed.

Mum smiled. "Well, what a big girl you are. Maybe you are old and wise enough to have your own phone, after all."

My eyes widened in delight. But just when things were becoming interesting in the getting-my-own-phone department, Dad came back into the room shaking his head.

"Tony, are you okay?" asked Mum.

"I can't believe it!" Dad rubbed at his bald head, as if he expected a genie to come out of it. "That was work on the phone, calling about me not going back to Norfolk."

317

"Is that a problem?" asked Mum, looking worried and making me worried.

Dad looked at us all very seriously. "Apparently, they've been so impressed with what I've achieved in the past six weeks, they've only decided to offer me a partnership position anyway!"

"Really?" asked Mum, sounding like one of **the Twinzies** when they've been offered sweets.

"Really, really," grinned Dad.

Mum's face lit up.

The Twinzies and I were confused. What did this mean? Did Dad have a job or not? Or did he still have to travel back and forth to and from Norfolk?

"Huh?" I finally said.

"It means, not only am I staying right here at my current job, but I get an even better promotion and a pay rise, which probably means extra Christmas presents for you lot!" boomed Dad.

"A puppy!" said Lena.

"A swimming pool!" called Peter.

"A puppy and a swimming pool —

and my phone!" I added, pushing my luck ever so slightly.

Mum and Dad looked at each other and burst out laughing.

Just then, someone started hammering at the front door.

Mrs Turner rose to her feet in fright.

My heart almost jumped clean out of my chest.

"What in the blazes?" cried Grampie Clive.

The clatter was so loud that Dad rushed to the door.

It was Auntie Sharon. She didn't look dressed for the date with her driving instructor. In fact, she was wearing the same clothes she had on from earlier, which was very unlike my aunt. Her sparkly Christmas wig was also slightly lopsided.

"Sharon? What's wrong?" asked Mum as she rushed to her sister.

Auntie Sharon was breathless as she spoke, as if she'd run all the way from her apartment to our house. Daz was hot on her heels.

"She's gone," Auntie Sharon spluttered. "She's packed her cases and gone. Is she here?"

Mum gasped and shook her head. "What do you mean, gone?"

Auntie Sharon, hands shaking, whipped a letter out from her Gucci handbag.

I didn't have a good track record with letters. This didn't feel good. Dad took it from her and started reading.

Sharon,

I have to go. I will explain later. All will become clear, but I've had the sudden urge to do something I should have done a while ago. You know that I'm a woman of impulse — and when I set my mind to something it has to be done. Speak soon.

Mother

This couldn't be true. She couldn't be gone. She'd just sung and performed like a mash-up of those old singers Aretha Franklin and Tina Turner. She'd been supping sweet hot chocolate with Mum. We were getting somewhere. No, this wasn't real. I didn't know whether to shout out in anger or cry.

"Just when I thought the leopard had changed its spots," tutted Mrs Turner.

Mum's body sagged as though she was a deflating hot-air balloon. "I'm sorry," she said and then she swept out of the room straight into the arms of...

...Glammy Pepper!

"Were you all born in a barn? Why is the front door butt-naked wide open?" was all Glammy said in that Jamerican accent of hers, as if she'd just nipped to Chanda's Groceries for some milk.

"Momma!"

"Glammy!"

"Miss Pepper!"

The cries rang out simultaneously.

It was as if we were witnessing the ghosts of Christmas past, present and future wrapped up in one very glamorous person.

"Can someone tell me what's going on?" demanded Mrs Turner as she threw herself down in shock without looking where she was sitting. But she soon got another shock, because she sat on the toy nutcracker soldier that

Peter had just left standing up on the sofa.

"Momma, I thought you'd gone. Like vamoosed out of here," cried Auntie Sharon.

"Oh, Sharon, darling, you can be so melodramatic. I don't know where you get it from."

We all stared at Glammy in disbelief.

She carried on without batting an eyelash. "I came to speak to Cheryl and ask if we could start again. I was on my way here in a taxicab, but we drove past the sweetest little boutique store, and I just *had* to stop and pick up a few more Christmas gifts for the children. I meant what I said, I'm here to stay come rain or shine — you can't get rid of me that easily. Plus, I couldn't fit all of my things in the taxi and give Sharon and Daz a ride."

Glammy went over to Mum and Auntie Sharon and held their hands. "Girls, I have never been the most conventional of mothers, that's true — and I'm sure not even you, Cheryl, would disagree with me on that."

Mum glared at Glammy Pepper in a way that said "you ain't wrong, girlfrien'".

"But if you can forgive me one more selfish act,

Cheryl," said Glammy. "I don't want to miss out on any more. I don't want this bad feeling to continue. Would you mind if I come back and stay to try and work things out?"

I must admit, I felt giddy with the shock of what was playing out in front of my eyes. Glammy was like a roller-coaster ride. Thrilling, exciting, yet ever-so-slightly shocking at the same time, but you just want to keep going back for more. I wondered what Mum would do now — get back on the ride, as she'd told me she would, earlier, or throw up on the spot and say never again.

Mum folded her arms and screwed up her face, but then unfolded them again as she looked over at me. Her face softened. "You're not easy, Mum, by any means, but I promised someone very special that I would try." Mum smiled at me gently and nodded. I smiled back and gave her the biggest thumbs up **EVER**.

"Whew, I'd raise a glass of punch to that, if I had one," sighed Grampie Clive, cracking his neck again.

"Lord, have mercy! May God forgive me in church on Christmas Sunday, but, Clive, I'd have a glass of rum punch too," cried Granny Cynthie. "But a cup of tea will have to do, if we can ever get Tony to make a pot."

"Pour one for me too, please, and make it strong," seconded Mrs Turner.

With that, Dad went to make the tea.

"What was all that about?" whispered Lena.

Peter shrugged. "Who knows? But I bet the presents that Glammy just bought are really goooood!"

The Twinzies gave each other a loud high-five and grinned wildly.

"MERRY CHRISTMAS!" they shouted.

"MERRY CHRISTMAS!" we all chorused.

Now, I hoped it could be.

40

CHRISTMAS RICHES

This would be our first Christmas without Grandad, but we tried to keep up the same traditions.

On Christmas Eve, we did our annual festive jive. It isn't a jive, like a Strictly Come Dancing kind of jive, it's just a long family walk we take around the neighbourhood.

The sky was still, and frost was fighting to keep hold of the ground. It had settled like icing sugar onto the roads and pavements, and spiderwebs, as delicate as shiny glass baubles, stretched from tree branches.

"It's itching to snow," said Mum, looking up and holding her hand to the grey sky.

"Ooh, I'm dreaming of a white Christmas," smiled Dad.

What is it with grown-ups and all this talk about the

weather? **The Twinzies** and me were even dressed for snow. I was boiling in my coat, woolly hat, and long scarf wrapped around my neck like a coiled snake. **The Twinzies** boing-ed along the pavement, like round beach balls, in their padded outfits. Mum insisted on layers just in case we were hit by a blizzard.

They continued to talk about the weather as we walked past our neighbours' houses. So many were decked out with beautiful decorations, waiting for night to fall before they sparkled into life.

Our festive jive was slightly different this year. We took a detour past Beeches Valley Country Park to Evie's house. Her family made us feel so welcome. We enjoyed eggnog and the grown-ups tasted Mr Evans's own special Christmas rum punch, and I finally got to meet Hannah-Jade, Evie's sister. Mum cooed over Claudette's warming drawer and two ovens, and they both started nattering away like they were old friends. They even shared their "jazzing up Brussels sprouts" recipes. I just had to hope they tried their recipes out on each other and not on me! Ugh!

Dad told everyone the "Sunshine was born in a taxi"

story that Grandad always used to tell about the day I was born. And Mr Evans got out his old grip from the garage and showed Mum and Dad his wooden toys from Jamaica. Evie and me even sat down and started piecing together one of her dad's old jigsaw puzzles — until we got a bit bored. Dad finished it off, but at least we tried!

Carl and Claudette invited us back round on New Year's Eve and said how happy they'd be to see in the new year with new friends.

For so long I'd worried about everything changing — how we'd manage without Grandad. But then there were other things I'd been worrying about that had got better. Miss Fairweather was actually okay after all. Riley had realized he'd made a mistake and owned up to it. Evie and me were proper friends. Glammy was here and staying put — and Mum was okay with that. Change, I realized, could be good too. And, as for going to high school? Well, we'd see. That was an adventure for another day.

On Christmas morning, we came downstairs to find

Glammy Pepper up, and Auntie Sharon and Daz, who had already come over to open presents with us. We tumbled into the living room and huddled around the Christmas tree, as if it was a roaring fire. And that's when I spotted envelopes tucked into the tree as white as papery lanterns. I immediately recognized the joined-up handwriting on the envelopes. Grandad!

I gulped as I opened my envelope ever so carefully, while **the Twinzies** hurriedly opened theirs.

We'd all been given money. Grandad always gave us money every Christmas. I couldn't believe he'd still thought about leaving us gifts, even when he was so sick. And this time, he'd also left a little note inside each envelope.

Sweet Sunshine, maybe you could use this as credit towards a new phone, hey? But be good, and don't nag your mum and dad too much, you hear?

Lena, if you're not able to get your puppy this year, don't worry, treat yourself to something nice and less yappy.

Peter, what is the harm of buying another toy? But make it a good one!

Dariuszkz, a big man like you has big-man things to buy. Shop wisely.

"Bless your old grandad," said Auntie Sharon with a sniff. "Even though he isn't with us, he's still all around. I've even kept up his tradition of buying his special Christmas lottery numbers." Auntie Sharon pulled out a piece of pink paper from her silver jumpsuit. She kissed it and slipped it back into her pocket.

After we'd opened our presents, I went and fetched the lucky penny that we'd found in the park and gave it to Auntie Sharon for extra luck with the lottery ticket. She smiled, rubbed it and placed it in her pocket.

I can't believe I'm saying this, but I was so happy that day, I'd even stopped worrying about whether I would get a phone. I even smiled about the orange, woolly cardigan that Mrs Turner had knitted for me. Somehow, just being together, along with the special envelopes from Grandad, meant I was, surprisingly, all right. For now.

"Hey, I can see a present tucked away behind the tree," said Dad. "If no one wants it I guess I'll just keep it for myself."

Dad picked it up. The present was a square shape. Not huge, that's why we'd probably missed it, but it was wrapped up in glistening silver paper with a white ribbon neatly tied around it. It looked...special. Dad looked at the name tag and then waved it backwards and forwards. "Oh no, it isn't for me at all," said Dad in fake disappointment. "It's got Sunshine's name written all over it." Dad smiled and handed me the present.

My eyes lit up.

I carefully unwrapped the gift, as if I was opening a box of dynamite.

And there it was...

Was it really?

Yes.

Yes, it was!

I felt my eyes prickle.

"Why are you crying, Sunshine? Is the box empty?" asked Lena.

I shook my head and cuddled the box to my chest. "No, it's not empty."

I looked up. Mum and Dad were beaming.

Mum laughed. "The phone won't work by keeping it in the box, you know!"

"I just want to remember the newness," I said, feeling foolish, but clutching the phone even tighter. "It's the best present **EVER**!"

"Knock yourself out with it on Boxing Day, but today is for family," said Dad, after ten minutes of me hugging MY new phone.

So, I pulled myself away and left it to charge while we enjoyed the rest of the day — playing games, pulling crackers, telling corny jokes, and having our turkey and rice and peas Christmas dinner, with all the trimmings (I left the sprouts). My brilliant Granny Cynthie had

 managed to bake another of her famous Christmas cakes and Grampie Clive's rum punch was served to the adults from the special punchbowl that was taken out of the big people's drinks' cabinet and used every Christmas.

As I passed Mrs Turner her second slice of cake, she held onto my hand.

"I've been observing you quite a lot lately, young lady," she said. "And I have something to say."

What was Mrs T going to say now? I hoped she didn't have one of her "little jobs" for me to do. Not on Christmas Day.

"You're growing into a fine young lady. You're a credit to your grandfather and he'd be very proud of you." Mrs Turner's voice wobbled.

"Thank you, Mrs Turner," I said. "Thank you ever so much."

"You're very welcome." She smiled as she munched into the slice of cake.

In the evening, we all settled down to watch some Christmas TV, and lolled around on the sofas and floor cushions. Even Glammy Pepper looked relaxed, like she wasn't ready to go catch a plane anywhere in a hurry. She sat with her legs stretched out on the pouffe, and her new golden, sparkly slippers, that **the Twinzies** and me had bought her for Christmas, gleamed in the lamplight.

Peter went over to the window and opened the blinds. A hazy, but bright, light shone through.

"It's snowing!" he called.

Sure enough, delicate flecks of snow floated down from the pale, evening sky and melted into the cold ground.

"Can we build a snowman tomorrow? There are some carrots in the fridge," said Lena.

"Yes, and we can use M&Ms for eyes! We can take them from Glammy's secret stash!" shouted Peter.

Mum gave Glammy and Peter one of her special looks.

"Oops," said Glammy and Peter at the same time.

And then Mum...

...smiled.

Dad craned his neck through the window and up to the

open sky. "It doesn't look like sticking snow, but if it does settle overnight, we'll make a snowman so big, it'll look like the Loch Ness monster has moved to the Midlands!"

Dad's eyes shone brighter that the night sky. I think he was looking forward to snowman-building more than **the Twinzies**. Grown-ups really do love the weather!

I, on the other hand, had my own plans for Boxing Day. I'd be in a group video call with Arun, Charley and Evie. I'd already written their numbers down ages ago in my **No Worries** notebook, desperately hoping that one day I'd be able to use them. Ooh, or maybe I could even video the snowman-building on my new phone and then call them. There are so many options when you're digital!

Glammy started humming a tune and then broke into an old song, called "Have Yourself a Merry Little Christmas". We were all lulled into a happy swaying motion by Glammy's singing, and it felt so warm and satisfying, as if we'd all sipped at a cup of hot chocolate, piled high with whipped cream, marshmallows and chocolate sprinkles.

I'd realized that worries will always come and go, but at this moment, life was the very best it could possibly be. You know, it did feel like a merry little Christmas after—

"ARRRRRGGGGHHHHHHHHHHHHHHHHH!" Auntie Sharon let out a blood-curdling scream.

Grampie Clive shot out of his chair like a jack-in-a-box. Miss Fairweather's exercises must have worked a treat because I hadn't seen Grampie move so quickly in years. "What in the blazes?" he shouted.

Auntie Sharon was fanning herself really quickly with her lottery ticket. I wanted to tell her there was no way anything as small as that would cool her down, but she was still too busy screaming — that is, until she started hyperventilating.

"Someone fetch her a paper bag to blow into!" commanded Glammy Pepper. "She's about to combust!"

"Sharon, what's happened now?" demanded Mum.

"Blouse and skirts! My old dad has come up trumps!" screamed Auntie Sharon, pointing at balls filled with numbers on the TV screen. "I've only just gone and scooped the jackpot. I've won the lottery!"

EPILOGUE

CHRISTMAS HOLIDAYS
(AND WAY PAST BEDTIME)...

Pudding Crew Group Chat

Sunshine: Christmas turned out to be really good, when I didn't expect it to be this year.

Arun: True. I'm sooooo tired though. My parents have been FaceTiming all our relatives and getting me to act out my audition piece for the School of Music and Dramatic Arts again and again. I'm a bit sick of Olaf now tbh. I've been having dreams about a bunch of angry snowmen running after me, waving their stick arms in the air. Until I fall off a cliff.

Charley: Oh.

Sunshine: Lol. They're just super happy for you.

Sunshine: I mean your parents are happy for you, not the snowmen in your dream. Obvs. I really hope you get into the school.

Arun: K — and thanks! 😊

Charley: Well, all I know is that the toilets were the best at Greenhill Academy, and I liked Katie and Bella, and Troy and Malik, when they walked us around. I'm really looking forward to going now. That's if I get in. My sisters can't scare me any more!

Evie: I loved Greenhill Academy, too. It's the not knowing where we'll end up that's the scariest for me, but deliciously exciting at the same time.

Arun: Everything's changing.

Charley: And what about our SATs next year? 😬

Sunshine: Well, I guess we'll just get our SATs done and then...PARTAAAYYY! 😎

Charley: Lol.

Evie: YES! YAY to PARTAAYS!

Sunshine: ALWAYS AND FOR EVER!

Charley: ALWAYS AND FOR EVER!

Arun: ALWAYS AND FOR EVER!

Sunshine: NEXT YEAR, HERE WE COME!!! ♥

Shaka Hislop

used the power of the individual
to make a change

Shaka can use these letters after his name, because he was awarded the gold Chaconia Medal for his performance in the World Cup. The medal is the second highest national award in Trinidad and Tobago

Neil Shaka Hislop CM knew from an early age that he wanted to play football, and as the tallest player on his first team, he was given the job of goalkeeper. After graduating from St Mary's College in Trinidad, getting an honours degree in Mechanical Engineering, and interning with space agency NASA, Shaka realized his dream and joined Newcastle United FC as a goalkeeper. You could probably call Shaka an intergalactic goalie!

Shaka has a long list of awards for his successful footballing career, but this isn't the only thing he is well known for. In 1996 Shaka helped to found the UK's leading anti—racism educational charity, Show Racism the Red Card.

SHOW
RACISM
THE
RED
CARD

Shaka's decision to help support the charity came after he experienced a racist incident. A group were shouting racist abuse at him, but they suddenly stopped when they recognized him as Shaka Hislop, the famous Newcastle United football player. Just like that, the group started asking Shaka for his autograph instead.

It was after this horrible experience that Shaka realized he could use his status as a role model and the power of football to help educate young people and challenge the racism he and so many other people have been subject to.

To this day, Shaka, fellow high-profile footballers and other sportsmen and women, are used as role models when Show Racism the Red Card's anti-racism workshops are delivered to young people and adults in schools, workplaces and events held at football stadiums.

Find out more about Show Racism the Red Card at www.theredcard.org

October marks Black History Month in the UK. Black History Month gives everyone in the UK the opportunity to share and celebrate the impact of Black heritage and culture in Britain.

The event started in the United States with Carter G Woodson, known as the "Father of Black History". Carter was born in Virginia in 1875, the son of former slaves. After studying hard, with limited opportunities, and gaining a PhD in history from Harvard University, Carter created the first Black History Week in 1926. A PhD is a BIG deal! It's a very high qualification that you study hard for and when you achieve it you can give yourself the title of Doctor.

PLUS, Harvard University, where Carter studied, is one of the most famous universities in the world. He was so clever!

Carter's Black History Week led to Black History month, which was officially recognized by the US government in 1976, and first celebrated in the UK in 1987.

Black History Month is now celebrated nationwide, and can focus on present Black trailblazers and historic Black pioneers across all areas of life, from art to science, literature to engineering, music and more! From the very first Black Britons who arrived in this country in Roman times, to the Windrush generation and beyond, Black people from Africa, America, the West Indies and elsewhere have been living, working, studying, creating and building in the UK for centuries.

Black History Month is important because Black History has often been overlooked or ignored even though Black people have lived in this country for a very long time. This special month is just one way to remember and celebrate the achievements and contribution of Black people in the UK from the past right up to the present day.

In Sunshine's classroom, lots of inspirational Black Britons are celebrated for Black History Month. Who would you include in your celebration?

Sunshine's
Cake Recipe

(Makes 12–14 slices)

Ingredients:

300g (11oz) plain flour

2½ teaspoons baking powder

2½ teaspoons ground cinnamon

½ teaspoon ground mace (optional)

A pinch ground allspice (optional)

150g (5oz) soft dark brown sugar

175ml (6floz) sunflower or vegetable oil

5 medium eggs

2 ripe, medium-sized bananas

1 tablespoon lemon juice

A 400g (14oz) can of crushed pineapple

For the frosting:

300g (11oz) full-fat cream cheese

125g (4½oz) icing sugar

You will also need a 20cm (8in) round, deep cake tin.

Method:

1) Heat the oven to 180°C, 350°F or gas mark 4. Grease and line the tin. Take the cream cheese out of the fridge.

2) Sift the flour, baking powder, cinnamon and allspice into a big bowl. Add the sugar and stir it in.

3) Put the oil in a bowl. Break an egg into a cup, then tip it into the oil. Do the same with each of the other eggs. Beat with a fork.

4) Peel the bananas and put them on a plate. Mash them with a fork or potato masher. Stir in the lemon juice. Then add the banana mixture to the oil mixture.

5) Set aside 1½ tablespoons of
the pineapple from the can. Tip
the rest of the contents of the can
into the oil mixture. Mix, then
pour this into the flour mixture.
Mix well. Scrape it into the tin.

6) Bake for 55–60 minutes, until risen and springy.
Test with a skewer. Leave in the tin for 10 minutes.
Turn it onto a wire rack. Leave until completely cold.
When the cake is cool, peel off the parchment.

7) For the frosting, put the cream cheese in a big bowl.
Beat until smooth, but don't beat too hard, or it will
become watery. Sift in the icing sugar. Add the pineapple
you set aside. Mix gently.

8) Put the cake on a serving plate. Spread the frosting
over the top and the sides, making peaks and swirls as
you spread it on. You could grate orange zest on top for
extra decoration.

ACKNOWLEDGEMENTS

So, I've actually finished my second book. Wow, how did that happen? Well, a bit like Rome, a book isn't made in a day (if only!). It takes a lot of (very special) people to help get those words into the right order and into readers' hands.

Thanks to Claire Wilson, who, even though she is now officially Agent of the Year, has always been my agent of the year. She is incredibly special and I'm so grateful and honoured that she represents me. Thanks also to Safae El-Ouahabi for her support.

The team at Usborne is remarkable. In the toughest of years for the company, they have worked so hard to help me complete this book. Thanks to Rebecca Hill, who must secretly be an octopus to achieve all she does. Thanks also to Stephanie King (I miss you!) and Alice Moloney (who is a dancing queen as well as a great editor). Katharine Millichope has worked wonders with the cover design — and I am so grateful to work with the extraordinary illustrator Fuuji Takashi. She just gets it — and gets the job done, brilliantly. And thanks to Asma Enayeh for the cuteness and humour you've brought to so many of the interior illustrations.

Fritha Lindqvist seems to fit 48 hours into one day and has propped me up many times when I've felt like falling down. She's just incredible.

Rawaa Elsir has been so helpful and encouraging. And, whatever I've needed, Beth Gardner has always been there to help. She's so calm and kind, even when I send her my badly filmed author videos. I can't name everyone who's supported me at Usborne (I'd simply run out of room), but needless to say, they are a brilliant writing family and I'm so proud to be published by them.

Colour PR has also done a wondrous job in supporting the book and getting it to shine in so many different – and wonderful – places, and I'm especially grateful that this has happened during the 75th anniversary year of HMT Empire Windrush's arrival to Britain. Thank you, Liz, Zekra and Dani.

The children's writing community is also very special. An army of bloggers, booksellers, librarians, reviewers and teachers read so many books – and work so hard – to get them into the hands of young readers. Special mentions to Kevin Cobane, Tom Griffiths, Scott Evans, Anne Thompson and Sarah Webb. They are just a few examples of the many book heroes who work wonders, every day, in promoting children's literature. Thanks to everyone who has reviewed, recommended Sunshine, and shown your support.

The Usborne Community Partnership is also fabulous. It was such a pleasure to attend one of their conferences in 2023 and to learn about their incredible commitment and passion.

Thanks also to Birmingham Stories (and the wider National Literacy Trust), the Federation of Children's Book Groups, and BookTrust for all their brilliant support. And thanks to all the authors who have taken the time to read Sunshine's story and offer supportive quotes — as well as to the debut writing groups of 2022 and 2023: so funny, wise and always helpful.

I still have a day job, so a big thank you to my line manager, Stuart, who has been so supportive, understanding and kind.

Thanks for ever more to the Most High and to my family and friends, who endure my constant questions, and random musings, with such good grace — and who are always there to offer advice, support — and to persuade people to buy my books!

Finally, thank you to all the readers — young and old(er) — who have embraced Sunshine and her friends and family, so wholeheartedly. You make every difficult day of writing worth it.

Thank you, with all my heart.

Look out for more adventures with

SUNSHINE SIMPSON